Dying in a St ry

Stories

Tahira Naqvi

TSAR

Toronto

We acknowledge the support of the Canada Council for the Arts for our publishing program. We also acknowledge support from the Ontario Arts Council.

Cover art by Rossitza Skortcheva.

Canadian Cataloguing in Publication Data

Naqvi, Tahira
    Dying in a strange country

ISBN 0-920661-86-6

1. Pakistanis – North America – Fiction. 2. South Asian Americans – Pakistan – Fiction I. Title.

PS3564.A68D94 2001   813'.54   C2001-930552-4

Printed in Canada by Coach House Printing.

TSAR Publications
P. O. Box 6996, Station A
Toronto, Ontario M5W 1X7
Canada
www.candesign.com/tsarbooks

To Ammi,
who is at my side still and will be with me forever,
loving and beloved as always.

Dying in a Strange Country

Sakina Bano was afraid. Afraid not of the fact that she was on an airplane larger than her house for the first time in her life, nor of travelling alone, companionless, on a twenty-two hour journey with four stops in cities she had not heard of before with names she could not pronounce correctly, although this was something that would surely crowd fear into the heart and mind of any sixty-nine year old widow. No, it was not the journey that troubled her. Why, when the plane lifted itself from the ground and the noise and vibration rattled her skull, it was not fear that laid its hand upon her heart, but an exhilaration, as if she were being lifted like a cloud toward the sky. No, her fear had little to do with such concerns.

"Son, I can't come," she had written to Asad. "I'm old, I want to take my last breath in my own country, and be buried among my own people. Tell me this, if I die there, what will happen to me?"

First Asad tried to scold her in his letters, telling her she was stubborn, childish. "What example are you setting for the others?" he wrote irately. Sakina Bano was amused when her son scolded her. How ridiculous to be drowned in a storm of anxiety over something like this, he reproached. Ridiculous? What did he, a young man whose whole life lay ahead of him like a stretch of fertile fields, know

1

of such things? Letter after letter fell into the tinny silence of her letterbox on 73 Sabir Street, Gujranwala. Then Asad gave her an ultimatum: he said pointblank he would not come home until she first visited him in Amreeka. "I had not imagined that you would deny me this little comfort, but you have and so I too will be stubborn," he added. She smiled to think that is what she often did, complain and give him ultimatums, but now it was his turn.

She relented. Dragging her fear along with her like a tenacious shadow, she boarded the plane and thought, "He'll never come back and live on 73 Sabir Street so I must now see where his new home will be. Everyone is talking about Amreeka,' I should see what's the fuss about."

A clinking, clattering noise interrupted her reverie. Within minutes the air in the cabin was redolent with the smell of richly spiced food, seasoned heavily with garam masala, like wedding fare. "We're going to eat," Sakina Bano told herself nervously. She wasn't hungry, having eaten dinner at Kubra's house an hour before her departure from Lahore. "Here Amma, just a little more, who knows what you'll get on the plane," her daughter had said, depositing another helping of pulao with green peas on her mother's plate.

The food carts began to crowd the aisles. Sakina Bano had been warned about the possibility of pork in airline food and elsewhere, and "I hear the meat isn't always halal," her daughter had said in a cautionary tone. There was also alcohol. She could smell it, like urine left overnight in the open drain along a street wall. Well, then she must ask, she could lose nothing by asking. But how difficult that was! Food trays were being passed with such rapidity that she found it impossible to hold the stewardess's attention long enough for a question. Also, she felt awkward, overcome by a diffidence she could not account for. Was she one who had difficulty speaking her mind?

Her tray remained untouched. She did not even try to slip her finger under the silvery wrapping and lift a corner to see what she was about to eat, and then, when coffee and tea were being passed out, she swiftly laid a restraining hand on the stewardess's arm. Her reserve disguised with a self-conscious smile, she asked in a small voice, "This is all halal meat, isn't it?"

"We serve only halal meat, Ammaji," the woman replied with a condescending inflection, her eyes, heavy-lidded from the weight of mascara and layers of green and blue makeup, flickering only momentarily with interest.

Rid of her dilemma, Sakina Bano turned to the food. She removed the silver foil on the tray and looked down, with surprise, on biryani and korma. Some of the buttery brown rice slipped onto her kurta front as she neatly rounded off small portions with her fingers, and after the first morsel was chewed and swallowed, she realized she was hungry after all. The food was well cooked, spicy, and although she would have preferred a fluffy, steaming chappati and some daal of maash, this was something to talk about when she returned to Sabir Street. Wedding food on the plane. Well, why not, after the thousands of rupees for one ticket.

As she wiped her hands later with a white paper napkin, she thought, What a waste. Could she not have walked to the bathroom and washed her hands? But where was the bathroom, could she easily walk to it? she asked herself in sudden consternation. "There will be many new things, Amma," Asad had written. "Just watch what the others are doing." No one was running to the bathrooms to wash hands, she saw.

On her left sat a dour-looking man, in his late sixties perhaps, or maybe older, with a stomach flabby like risen dough and a peppery, bristly beard, and she wasn't about to learn anything from watching him. He was probably as much a novice as she; he had dropped cutlery at least twice and his paper napkin was lying forlornly on the floor while he used his handkerchief to wipe his hands. But now the young girl on her right, in the window seat, who had told Sakina Bano earlier that her name was Abida and she was returning to college, now she seemed like a person who had made this trip more than once. She had handled the paper napkin deftly, making no fumbling moves with the cutlery that came wrapped in a narrow plastic bag.

3

Sakina Bano briefly fidgeted with the bag in the hopes of getting a spoon out, but she soon discovered she would have to wrestle with it before she gained access to what was buried inside. Why, who needed the spoon, and anyway, was she going to flounder clumsily with a fork and knife and make herself look foolish? She had enough sense not to reveal her shortcomings. So she ate as she had always done, with her fingers. The lissome young girl with bright, almond-shaped eyes and long, black hair that fell on her shoulders like strands of silk, was Pakistani, and therefore no stranger to old customs.

But what was all this compared to the cacophonous noise that clamored in her head? That threatened to drown out all other sounds?

What if . . . yes, what if she suffered a heart attack just this instant and died? Why, don't people often die quietly and without a fuss? And if she were a corpse, would the airline transport her back to Pakistan? What if the plane was forced to make a landing in the country they were flying over when she took her last breath, and her body was abandoned there, in a strange country? She knew Cairo was their first stop, but were they near Cairo? She couldn't be certain. However, the thought that Egypt might be the place where she was left for burial provided some comfort, for at least then she would be among fellow Muslims.

Sakina Bano swallowed the spit in her mouth which felt like a cotton ball, leaned back in her seat, her hand firmly wrapped around the hot cup of tea in front of her. She took a deep breath. For the moment, just for the moment, the fear was put to rest.

Cairo was a hurried stop. The passengers were not allowed to get off; something about terrorism, she heard one of the passengers remark. She imagined men rushing about with guns, spraying strangers with bullets and felt unnerved by sudden dread. But to die was to die. She smiled the smile of a fatalist. What was important was where one died. What could a terrorist do to her in Cairo?

After Cairo she lost track of time. Day and night seemed to cross over so rapidly she didn't know whether to sleep or remain awake.

When the plane came down at Frankfurt it was nearly morning she saw. Below her, when the plane descended in sudden swoops as if it were about to fall, were dark smoky whorls streaked with orange and red and fringed with gold.

Inside, the airport looked isolated, the only passengers in sight wandering about like mindless creatures, faces ashen from exhaustion and lack of sleep, their bodies slouched with fatigue, their steps leaden. Some were stretched out on shiny, slippery benches in the transit lounge to snatch whatever fitful sleep they could. Airport officials, usually crisp and alert no doubt, also wore crestfallen looks and moved about unhurriedly. The clock on a white wall above a red sign she couldn't read said three.

No sooner did she deposit her weary, aching body into one of the chairs that lined a large glass wall than a tiny spurt of anxiety crawled out of her thoughts like a worm, edged its way into her blood, spreading like an arrhythmic flurry. What if? The possibility was too frightful for her to weigh. Sakina Bano stiffened in her chair. She must not fall asleep. Her eyes strayed to the clock, she looked for the seconds hand. But the hand was stationary, it seemed, stilled. A German clock keeping German time; what could it mean to her? Turning away, she looked about her anxiously and observed Abida, her young companion from the plane, slumped in a seat not too far from her. Her thin arms crossed over a large canvas bag in her lap, the girl slept soundly. How Sakina Bano envied the untroubled and tranquil expression on her face. How happy her dreams must be, unencumbered and free.

Later, back on the plane, before the food carts came clattering down the aisles again, Sakina Bano decided she would talk to Abida. The two women reminisced about places they both knew in Lahore, Abida's hometown; Anarkali Bazaar where every day men, women, and children roamed about as if a carnival was in progress, Bano Bazaar where a woman may find all she ever wanted, McLeod Road where all the cinema houses were and where mammoth film posters rose like walls guarding a city, and the shrine of Data Sahib where you made vows and prayers were answered.

5

"Is this your first visit, Ammaji?" the girl asked, placing the book she had been reading face down in her lap.

"Yes," Sakina Bano said, sighing wistfully. "My son has been asking me for a long time, but it's not easy you know, Kubra, my daughter, was having her first baby, and then the house had to be whitewashed before the rains. Asad, my son, lives in Dan-bury, Con-necti-cut." Her lips stretched back, her tongue rolling, she emphasized each syllable as Kubra had instructed her. Such difficult names. "And where are you going?"

"I live in New York City," Abida replied, searching the older woman's face for a glimmer of recognition, "a place called Manhattan. It's not too far from Danbury, your son will know where it is. Your son's married?"

"No, but Kubra and I have found a girl for him. If he likes her we will have the wedding next year." She rubbed her forehead with her fingers in a nervous gesture and lowered her head. "If I'm still alive then," she muttered sadly, her face turned away.

The girl's eyes widened in alarm. "You're not sick, Ammaji, are you?"

Sakina Bano shook her head and smiling sheepishly, lifted a hand and gesticulated. "No, no, I'm not sick, except for the pain in the legs, in my back, the cataracts that keep growing too fast. No, but old age is a kind of sickness too, isn't it, child? I only pray my maker allows me to die in my own country." Sakina Bano felt immense relief after this confession.

"You shouldn't talk like this Ammaji. In America men and women in their seventies get married and start new lives." Abida smiled mischievously.

"Ai hai, child, what nonsense is this? And when do they prepare for death? Or is it that they think they will live forever? New attachments, new pain, who wants it all over again?"

Abida broke into a laugh. Sakina Bano wondered if the young woman could help. "Child," she whispered with her hand resting on Abida's arm, "tell me this, what happens if someone dies? I mean how do they bring the body back?" She was intent on knowing the truth, all of it, however ugly and menacing.

"What?" Abida turned to her in surprise. Then, realizing her companion was serious, she said, "Ammaji, I don't know too much about these things, but I'm sure arrangements can be made to transport the body. Actually I think four airline tickets have to be bought. It's expensive, I've heard. But you know, Ammaji," she looked at Sakina Bano solicitously, "nowadays there are burials right there in special cemeteries that have been allotted by Muslim communities."

This piece of information proved distressing. There was little solace in what the girl said. Asad could never afford four tickets, and then she'd have to be buried in . . . Dan-bury! Sakina Bano collapsed in her seat, her spirits fallen, her desire to continue the conversation waned.

Perhaps he can get a loan, she brooded over her next cup of tea. Surely it would be a burden, but he could have all of her savings, nearly fifty thousand rupees, and all the other property would be his anyway. She will not mind, although her husband's soul would be agitated, it's been in the family for nearly sixty years, but Asad could sell the house on 73 Sabir Street and invest the money, and there was also some agricultural land that had belonged to Asad's grandfather. The picture began to appear a little less bleak. She arranged a pillow behind her head and settling into a comfortable position, shut her eyes.

"At the airport, keep your wits about you," Asad had shouted into the phone. Although he had described the airport to her in detail, at Kennedy Airport she was still like a child lost among strangers in a crowded bazaar. Her son's instructions were explicit: "Have your passport in your hand when you're in line at Immigration, stay close to people from your flight, if you're in doubt ask someone, ask Amma, don't be afraid to ask. At customs, open your suitcases quickly if told to, but don't volunteer, tell the officer what you're carrying if he inquires, and please, Amma, don't bring mangoes. Carrying fruit is not permitted." Instructions or no instructions, she

7

was on her own, she realized with sudden panic.

At customs a tall, thin man with a deeply lined, ashen-white face, thin red nose and probing eyes pointed to her suitcase and asked her if she had any mangoes. She knew the English word. She shook her head, secretly wondering if he would question her further. Deep inside her suitcase, carefully wrapped in a plastic bag were two bottles of pickled mangoes that she had prepared with her own hands. The small, dark green, tart mangoes she had taken down from her own tree growing in the front garden. No, he didn't want to know more. Anyway, snug in those bottles was not fruit, just tiny pickled raw mangoes that Asad favored.

Afterward, a dark, stocky man, distinguishable from the others by a uniform he wore, silently piled her two cases along with Abida's on a large trolley, and signaling them, strode toward gray double doors that seemed to dominate a seemingly endless white wall.

Beyond the doors, around the corner, was Amreeka. Never before had Sakina Bano seen so many people gathered in one place. Not even on Eid shopping days in the bazaars when the city's inhabitants spilled into the streets as if a catastrophe had forced them to suddenly vacate their homes. So different from each other, the people here milled about restlessly, speaking languages that seemed like babbling noises to her. Some of the people looked familiar, men, women and children from either India or Pakistan, but there were also others who must be from countries she was aware existed on a map, a geography of strangeness.

The two women followed the dark man in the uniform. As she lifted a trembling hand to adjust the slipping dupatta from her head, Sakina Bano felt overcome by a wave of dizziness, and if she hadn't caught on to the railing on her left she might have stumbled and fallen. Where is Asad? she wondered, gnawed by anxiety, and suddenly, feeling his attentive gaze upon her, she spotted him. He rushed toward her, his face drawn and his brow creased with concern, as if she were a child who had gone away and was returning.

Once they were outside, Abida said goodbye to her and got into a car with a young man who couldn't be much older than she. Her brother? Her husband? Maybe just a friend. Sakina Bano waved, saddened by the thought that she would probably never see her again.

It was cool. The sky was a dark blue. She saw stars. In the midst of all the strangeness the sky seemed to afford a sense of comfort, for was it not the same sky she saw every night in Gujranwala, now thousands of miles away? Her fear receded as she trudged alongside her son, her hands nervously clutching a corner of her dupatta.

*

Asad's apartment was small. Just one bedroom. Barely enough space for a low, three-drawer bureau and a bed that had no headboard and shook and rattled as if it had a loose bottom when you sat on it. The kitchen, tiny and doorless, was the size of a bathroom in her house, and the area between the bedroom and the kitchen her son had set up as the drawing room with one upholstered sofa not very clean, a low table scratched and marked with circular cup stains, and two chairs on which the paint was peeling untidily. Is this what he had come to Amreeka for? He had left the long, circular veranda of 73 Sabir Street, the spacious rooms with elevated, beamed ceilings and windows everywhere, the wide, open red-brick courtyard with the large mulberry tree where the winter sun warmed you and where you slept under dark blue starry skies on hot summer night. For this? There must be something she could not see as yet, something that eluded her because she was old and because her mind was clogged with uneasy thoughts.

On a Friday, nearly a week after her arrival in Danbury, Sakina Bano accompanied her son to what he informed her was the local Islamic Center. Having envisioned, if not a mosque, at least a place which had some trappings of the Islamic, she was stupefied by what she saw.

"This is the Salvation Army Church," Asad whispered in her ear as the two of them entered a long passage where she was greeted by dark-haired children shrieking playfully, many of them running, chasing the others. As she drew her dupatta about her, a girl no older than seven or eight, her plaits ribboned, her eyes wide with excitement, ran into her and almost fell. Sakina Bano bent over quickly to hold her, buffing the girl's fall with her arm. The girl looked up at her, stiffened and moved away awkwardly.

A church, she wondered in amazement. Muhammad and Issa in the same place! What would her husband say if he were alive? She saw a few women. Some wore shalwar and kameez, three others were in long robes with scarves covering their hair. Who are these women? Sakina Bano wondered. Egyptian, Saudi, maybe Iranian? A group of men stood in the narrow passage; removed from the women, many young like her son, a few older and gray-haired with somber and wearied faces, they talked in low voices.

Not used to being in the company of strange man, unless she was in the bazaar or on a train or the bus stop, Sakina Bano felt uncomfortable when Asad introduced her to the people in the passage. Of course he wants them to know his mother has come to visit him in his new home, she thought, trying to placate herself.

"Walekumsalaam, walekumsalaam," she mumbled with her head lowered as she sidled away from their intrusive attention. Asad led her to a room where more women sat, most of them tending infants.

Asad introduced her. A woman, who reminded her of Abida because of her boyish figure, long hair open to her shoulders and was younger than all the rest, came forward quickly to greet her. Soon all of them engulfed her excitedly as if she were a special guest.

"Do you like Amreeka?" a plump, attractive woman with a chubby baby on her arm, asked genially. She was rocking a baby who, his head lolling on her shoulder, drooled on the sparkling gold bangles on her wrist.

"Yes, yes, I like it, what is there not to like?" Sakina Bano wondered if any of them knew anything about transporting bodies by air.

"You must come and visit us soon," the plump woman said, smiling again, and before Sakina Bano could respond to her invitation, the child began to whimper and the young woman walked away, patting the infant and cooing softly.

Her name, Sakina Bano soon discovered, was Husna, while the one who resembled Abida was Sabiha. They were all so eager, these women. Eager to be friendly, to be hospitable, and as they talked their solemn enthusiasm lighted up their faces, imbuing their voices with energy so that the most trivial topics of conversation seemed to assume undue importance. One day Asad's wife will be here, among them, first alone and then with a child on her arm, while on Sabir Street, Sakina Bano will wait out her days by herself, expecting the postman's rattle at the letterbox, running out for letters, for photographs charting the progress of her daughter-in-law, her new grandchild.

The children were assembling for class. One of the men, fair skinned, with a beard that was black like the overused surface of a tawa, a short, chubby man no more than thirty-five or thirty-six, came in and started talking to the children. Why, Arabic is his mother tongue, Sakina Bano realized with surprise. When he began reciting from the Koran, how buoyantly the words of the ayaats fell from him, like unhurried rain from the heavens.

"He's from Egypt," Asad told her later. Class was being held in a section of the large hall in which everyone was congregated, and separated from the place where the women sat by a tall, movable partition. The women in the long dresses and scarves had come in too, and Sabiha chatted energetically with them in English. Asad and the other men had moved in somewhere behind the partition as well; perhaps on the other side was another movable wall.

Her attention was suddenly snagged by the drop of a word that wiggled its way into her consciousness and was suspended there. Like a kite trapped precariously in the branches of a tree. Because she had been deeply engrossed in the melodic recitation, she missed the first part of the conversation, but the word "buried" didn't elude her. She turned to a slightly older woman, closer to her in age perhaps, her hair thickly patched with gray, large glasses with thick, opaque lenses hiding nearly all of her diminutive nose, who was now talking.

11

". . . she had cancer so her family knew she didn't have too long to live, and her son didn't take her back to Pakistan when she passed away. It was a Sunday, and all the stores were closed. Do you know, they couldn't even buy white cotton for her shroud? Isn't it just terrible?" She shook her head gravely and chafed her hands together.

"What did they do?" It was Husna, the baby now asleep with its head resting peacefully on her shoulder, the small pink mouth open.

Sakina Bano's heart convulsed. The ground seemed to slip from under her feet. She held her breath. Her gaze was riveted on the older woman's face.

"What can I say, it was just dreadful. May Allah save us from such a fate. All the friends of the family donated whatever new white bed sheets they had, and the women made a kaffan. She was buried in the town cemetery. Thank God there was a Turkish maulvi who could say the burial prayers."

Sakina Bano's mouth went dry. She felt sweat rise like tiny thorns on her skin. A thousand little invisible insects seemed to have set down their furry legs upon her person, and were moving, slowly. Bedsheets! What an unfortunate woman. And what guarantee they were all cotton? Wash and wear is what they are making these days. And to be buried among strangers—such a dismal fate. Poor woman, to be so far from home and die. To be wrapped in bed sheets which said, on small tags somewhere, "Made in Amreeka." Will the angels condescend to enter a grave where a body lay draped in a shroud made by Christians? Sakina Bano shuddered at the possibility of being abandoned by God's messengers at the hour of reckoning.

Conversation veered off to other subjects, but Sakina Bano remained entangled in a web of irreversible anxiety. Later that night, agitated and unsolaced, she tossed and turned on her bed as if she was on live coals. Sleep evaded her. Finally she decided to pray and sat on the janamaz with her prayer beads for a long time.

"Ya Allah," she entreated with outstretched hands, "I ask you only this. Let me return to my home, and then my life is yours to do what you want with it. I have no fear of death. I ask not to live forever. But

Dying in a Strange Country

there is great fear in my heart of dying here. In your infinite mercy grant me this one wish and I will never want anything for myself again."

She didn't know when she dozed off, the words gathering thickly on her tongue like molasses, but clear in her head. When she fell forward on the prayer mat she woke up with a start. Extending both arms out, she slowly brought the edge of the mat toward her, folding the rest of it as she rose to her feet slowly. It was time to sleep.

*

Sunny and humid, the day was warm, but nothing like a warm day in Gujranwala. The temperature there must have already climbed to a torrid, pasty hundred-and-two degrees. Here, it was pleasant. With the car windows down, a small breeze quietly fanned her face, making her drowsy.

She could not pronounce the name of the place Asad was taking her to. They were on their way to visit her niece Zenab, her cousin's daughter, a dear girl who always visited her in Gujranwala even though it was an out of the way town, always bringing gifts. Today Sakina Bano was taking her a hand-blocked brick-red tablecloth and a set of matching napkins. She knew what Zenab liked. And for Zenab's husband she had brought a vest that all the young men were wearing these days, and for the year-old baby it was an embroidered cotton kurta and pajama.

Sakina Bano would soon be asleep, except that the leafage astounded and mesmerized her and she had to constantly move her head to see it all. Never had she seen such density of foliage. Of such variety. No two trees seemed alike. Like walls, they rose on either side of the road until the sky, when she gazed up, was only a narrow strip of sharp, unclouded blue. Like a clear well-lighted path.

Something seemed to grasp at her attention when Asad stopped the car at one of the traffic lights. She glanced to her right and stared in wide-eyed wonder at the image before her. A hill, sloping lazily upward from the edge of the road, carpeted with grass so finely clipped it was like a velvet mantle, greener than any green she had ever known. Fresh, washed color interlaced with a trellis of sunlight filtered through tall trees lining the hill's highest borders. And little clusters of the brightest, sharpest red flowers, each cluster attended by a small, squat slab of gray stone. Sakina Bano gasped at the beauty of what she saw.

The question was squelched as soon as it raised its head in her thoughts. She knew the place. The perfect little slabs of stone had a voice that fell plainly into her ears. The car was moving again, and Sakina Bano fell against her seat as if she had travelled a great distance on foot and must rest now to catch her breath.

Her eyes shut, she found herself in another dwelling, a portion of land where her husband and so many of her relatives were resting. Dismal, overgrown with weeds and wildly tangled shrubbery, the only color was brought into the place by those who came to visit the graves. A red tinge from a dupatta here, a green kurta, a dab of purple chador, a brightly white cotton shirt, spotless like a new shroud. The earth here was dry, cakey and cracking, gashed where the pressure from the countless heavy stone mounds had dragged it open. The ocher of the earth presented no other hue. The trees that bent over the crumbling graves in postures of despair, were thin and untended, their spindly branches forever bare and shriveled. Spring seemed not to touch them, even lightly. It was like a place forgotten, by time, by nature, by life. The tall brick wall that enclaved the cemetery and which half stood and half fell, as everything else did there, seemed to shut out nature's benevolence just as it shut out the living world.

Sakina Bano moved restlessly in her seat. She emitted a long sigh.

"Amma, are you all right?" Asad cast a worried glance at her.

"Yes, yes I'm all right," she lied. How could she bring herself to tell him she wished she would be as fortunate as her husband. That she longed to be buried like him in the cemetery where earth had lost color. Her father was also there and her mother, her uncles and also her grandparents. There, she would not be alone.

She was assailed by fear again. Words in your head are like

dreams; no one knows of them except you, the dreamer. She must let her son hear the words that milled through her thoughts like a winter dust storm, thick, suffocating, cleaving through what stood in its path. She had made up her mind.

"Asad?" she said casually, as if she were going to ask him about Zenab's husband, whether he had decided to go back to Pakistan after he finished his training, or whether the baby had begun teething.

"Yes Amma?"

"Listen, now don't get upset . . ." Her voice cracked.

"What is it? Are you feeling all right?" Asad slowed down and she thought he might stop. So much traffic around them, he might get into an accident. What a burden she was, and she wasn't even dead as yet.

"I said I'm fine, I just want to discuss something, now don't get worried." She patted his arm and cleared her throat. "If something were to happen . . ." she increased the pressure on his arm as he opened his mouth to protest. "If, if something should happen, I want you to send me back to Pakistan." There. The words had escaped, ponderous, no longer erasable.

Shaken for a moment, he shook his head. "Amma, what kind of silly talk is this?" he said irritably. "Are you still carrying that absurd notion in your head? By God's grace you're healthy and there's no reason to suppose anything will happen." He was angry at her obstinacy.

"Don't get upset, son, you must understand, you can't get upset. I'm serious." She pleaded tearfully.

A smile appeared on his face. "Amma, Amma," he chuckled, "what's the matter with you?" Aware that she had not taken kindly to his humor he assumed a straight face. "All right, I promise, I promise. Are you satisfied?" His eyes pinned on the road, he struggled again with a smile.

"I think you will have to buy two tickets."

"What?" He turned again, to look at her in amazement this time.

She continued. "Keep your eyes on the road. You might have to get a loan because you need forty thousand rupees to send a body back to Pakistan, but don't worry, I've got fifty saved in my account in Pakistan, and it's all yours."

Asad started to laugh, catching himself when she sniffled and tugged at his sleeve.

"I said I am serious. Why are you laughing? Promise you won't bury me in—what's the place called—Dan-bury." With a corner of her dupatta she wiped the tears on her cheeks.

"I promise, Amma," Asad said in an apologetic tone.

"Promise you will take me home to Sabir Street." She clutched her son's arm.

"Yes, I will," her son said earnestly, "I promise."

Sakina Bano blew her nose with her handkerchief and leaned back in her seat. The strip of blue sky seemed to have vanished. The branches of trees formed a crested canopy, hiding the sky from her. Feeling weightless, as if a cumbersome burden she had been carrying all this time had suddenly dislodged itself, she shut her eyes. Her thoughts, which only moments ago held her down like a chain of steel, became amorphous and flew inside her head, like a kite cut off from its restraining cord, free.

Thank God for the Jews

On a morning like any other August morning with its promising bright sunshine, its summer aura of capricious warmth so unlike the faithful torrid heat of August mornings in Lahore, Ali said, "Asad is bringing his mother over for dinner tomorrow."

"Sakina Phupi? When?" Zenab asked in alarm, forgetting how many teabags she had dropped into the small white Corningware teapot. Five would be too many and three not enough. She peered anxiously into the pot and counted: three were clearly visible, the fourth could be an illusion. With a swift movement of her hand she tore off a Tetley tag and threw in another teabag. The water gurgled with a familiar sound as she poured it from the kettle into the teapot, steam rising to embrace her face warmly. "But she said on the phone she was going to be in New Jersey with cousin Abid for another week!" Her voice rose almost to a scream.

"She must have changed her mind," Ali said calmly, ignoring the panic in her voice. "Anyway, she's back with Asad. He called me yesterday at the hospital and I told him Sunday would be fine." Ali was speaking from the bedroom now. He thought nothing of starting a serious conversation with her when he was not in the same room with her, a habit that had turned into an annoyance, a little thing in a bag of innumerable little things that she had to muddle through.

Zenab didn't know whether she should be glad at the prospect of seeing her cousin Asad, a young man who laughed unreservedly at Ali's jokes and ate her food as if he had tasted none better, or be excited at the thought of meeting Sakina Phupi, who would bring her fresh gossip about the relatives in Lahore, or be upset that her husband hadn't consulted with her before giving Asad the go-ahead for dinner. After all, preparations had to be made.

The kitchen was a picture of chaos. Unwashed plates in the kitchen sink, two Faberware pots crusty with overcooked spices from last night's cooking, jars of baby food, assorted Beechnut juices, cans of formula stacked untidily on the cramped Formica counters, the stove streaked with a combination of grease and gravy stains. She had allowed herself to be lazy. Unmindful of her wifely duties, last night when Ali left for the hospital at eleven to attend to an emergency, she settled comfortably on the sofa in the living room to watch the Eleven O'Clock Movie on channel 9. *The Snows of Kilimanjaro.* Ah . . . Gregory Peck, who had laid siege to her daydreams when she was a teenager and when romance seemed like life's greatest gift. Ah . . . even now he smiled, cocked his head to one side, furrowed his brow and Zenab wished she were Ava Gardner. Nobody's going to come and inspect my kitchen at this hour of night.

She had waved the kitchen away and out of her thoughts.

Leaving the tea to steep under the only teacozy she possessed, Zenab walked into their bedroom determined to let her husband know she wasn't altogether comfortable about Sakina Phupi's impending visit. She found him thrashing through a drawer, searching impatiently for clean underwear.

"But that's tomorrow," she wailed, picking up his white cotton pajama and kurta from the bedroom floor with one hand, his discarded socks with the other.

"Yes," Ali replied briefly without looking at her. Now he was rummaging for socks.

He's already beside a patient, no doubt. Taking a pulse. The round ends of the stethoscope snug into the little cavities of his ears, the world shut out. Playing God with such a casual air, nonchalantly. A face I don't know, don't understand.

She turned to straighten the pillows, tugged at the bed sheets and he was gone from there.

"And she'll eat only halal meat!" Zenab ran after him as if she were afraid he would run from her and be lost. In the kitchen now, he was pouring himself a cup of tea.

"We don't have any in the freezer?" he asked between quick gulps of tea, seemingly unmoved by her anxiety.

Uff! Gulping tea again. It's not mango squash. Sip it, slowly, savor it.

His long, dark brows formed uneven waves over his nose as he picked up a piece of toast and, taking a bite, began crunching noisily.

"Of course we don't," she said, desperation creeping into her voice. "We bought a couple of pounds of beef and half a dozen pieces of chicken from Halal Meats last month when we went to see *Mughal-e-Azam* at the Bombay Theater. Remember? It's all gone."

Sometimes Zenab and Ali bought halal meat, meat prepared the Islamic way, at one of the many Pakistani shops that lined the streets in Jackson Heights. Every once in a while they also ventured into the cramped, busy butcher shop called Halal Meats on Lexington in Manhattan, right next door to Naghma House where she and her husband spent hours searching for and buying records and tapes of old Indian songs. But generally it was beef, chicken, and lamb from the Grand Union down the road for them. Packed in shiny, neat packages that gave the impression that someone had gone through a great deal of trouble to give the shoppers only the best, the meat always had a fresh, clean look about it, and the packages were so easy to pick up and throw without too much thought into the shopping cart. Whenever she remembered to, Zenab recited "There is no God but Allah and Muhammad is his prophet," while she rinsed the meat with cold water. Making the effort to undertake that little ritual made her feel pious and wise.

19

"It's not like we'll be giving her pork," she protested. "Once we've said the kalima while washing the meat, it's okay, isn't it? Abba says the Koran doesn't say anything about how to prepare the meat, he says the kalima is enough. That's all I do. All this nonsense about bleeding the animal or pronouncing the name of Allah at the time the poor animal is put to the knife—it's ridiculous!" Frustration hung in her head like the beginnings of a migraine and she realized she hadn't had any tea yet; also, this wasn't a good time to engage her husband in a discussion about rational approaches to the preparation of meat.

He finished his second cup of tea and vigorously rubbed down the corners of his mustache with a paper napkin. "Your father's a rationalist, Zenab," he finally said. "But we both know there's more to Islam than what's in the Koran. Anyway, that's not the point. In Pakistan, you ate only halal meat, didn't you?"

"Yes," she conceded lamely, "but this is different . . ." Why? he might ask. She knew why, but . . . well, there wasn't enough time to explain.

"You know, my dear," he started again, trying to placate her but succeeding instead only in making her feel worse, "some people are more conservative, they don't want to compromise, they'll eat halal wherever they go."

"I know," Zenab said glumly.

"Let's see, what about fish?"

They were standing in the foyer now, his hand reaching for the doorknob.

Is he going to kiss me or is he going to forget?

"Fish?" Zenab leaned over to brush a tiny crumb that dangled invitingly from his dark, thick mustache.

True, fish was not subject to the same stringent laws as other types of meat. It had probably been spared because there wasn't any blood to contend with. What else could it be? But she had such bad luck with fish, always. Whenever she tried to fry fillets dipped in gram flour batter, the batter crumbled and separated from the fish the moment the piece was dropped into the bubbling, hot oil. Curried fish suffered a worse fate; no sooner had she turned the soft, white cubed chunks over than the chunks disintegrated, into mush. Usually she just threw everything into the garbage and started all over again with something else. If her mother saw her she would cringe at her wastefulness.

"Fish?" She looked at Ali closely to make sure he wasn't teasing. "In the first place I don't make very good fish, and in the second place how many kinds of fish are we going to serve? Who knows, maybe Sakina Phupi is allergic to fish." No one in Pakistan was allergic to fish.

"Well, I doubt that. Go ahead, love, try the fish, it's not that bad." He nodded encouragingly.

Surely he's desperate. He doesn't want to upset Sakina Phupi. And what tales she might take back with her. They've already forgotten their ways. Imagine not eating halal. What will it be next, pork?

"Okay, I'll try the fish, but don't blame me if it's a disaster. I hope they have some fresh cod at Grand Union, that's the only kind that works well in a curry. I'm not trying the frying recipe," Zenab threatened.

"All right, all right, and don't forget to use some oregano." He glanced at the clock on the living room wall, tweaked her cheek and was out the door with a smile and a "Bye," before she could ask, "But what do you know about oregano?" It probably reminded him of something his mother had used in her fish recipe, perhaps ajwain, she thought with some irritation. Did she even have ajwain?

He forgot to kiss me.

Left alone, Zenab dawdled in the foyer as if she were a guest in her own house. A glance at the yellow and beige linoleum revealed scuff marks made by her baby's walker; looking above she glanced upon the throng of cobwebs that looped with silken finesse in two corners of the white ceiling. She must do some cleaning this afternoon. Her two-year-old son, impervious to the trivialities and banalities of custom and habit gone awry in Westchester County, was still asleep.

From the kitchen, tea beckoned as a deliverer's promise would. All else must wait and be taken care of after this one cup of Tetley tea, a brand which had become her choice after a protracted dalliance with the likes of Earl Grey and other exotic brands; the Americans had done something right with tea after all.

With her cup cradled in her palms, she came into the living room and pulled down the shades from force of habit to shut out the morning sun, turned on the TV, and sat down on the settee. The warmth from the first sip slunk down her throat and made her feel good, sure of herself. She took another sip and crossed her legs.

The Eight O'clock News had begun. The Jews and the Muslims were fighting again in the Middle East. A tall, handsome reporter, who, with his upturned coat collar and straw-colored, windswept hair, seemed to belong in an ad for Burberrys in the *New Yorker,* was saying something about "recent acts of terrorism" in an insouciant voice. An Israeli school bus had been bombed. Its carcass sat forlornly on a hill; some children had been killed, some injured. A girl, perhaps only three or four years older than her son, ran away wildly from the soldier who scrambled after her to hold her. The camera moved with sudden abruptness to another scene before he had caught up with her. An Arab village in ruins. Nearly all the houses had been demolished, the survivors of the attack moving in slow motion like wandering spirits. An old woman, whose face looked oddly familiar, squatted before a crumbled, hollowed-out dwelling and cried without restraint, her mouth hanging open in a grotesque caricature of a smile.

During a commercial break Zenab decided to make a list so she wouldn't forget anything when Ali took her to Grand Union this evening. She scribbled "oregano."

Now I know. The old woman in the news. Crying in despair. She resembles Sakina Phupi. Saddened by loss and despair, all old women look the same.

Sakina Phupi was Zenab's father's cousin. Last summer, when Zenab visited her in Pakistan, she had confessed secretively that she missed Asad and at night lay awake thinking how she had never imagined he would be so far away, so inaccessible. The days were worse, especially now that she had lost her husband and her daughter was married and living in Rawalpindi. "A daughter-in-law will bring life into this house again," she said in a quavering voice. Zenab wondered why Sakina Phupi had chosen to blur the fact that her son was in America and that's where her daughter-in-law would be too, when she arrived on the scene. Her house would be forever what it was now. Still and haunted with memories. But she listened quietly as Sakina Phupi told her Asad had been begging her to come to America for a visit. Her aunt's eyes, set far into their sockets and glazed over with age, filled quickly with tears. "Don't say anything to him," she entreated, wiping with her dupatta the moisture that had trickled thickly over her grooved, leathery cheeks. "But you must come Phupi ji," Zenab had said, "why are you so reluctant to come?" Zenab knew her aunt was biding her time, waiting until her son begged. Her mother would do the same. In a mother's love too there's revenge, not always sweet.

Still feeling unsure about fish, Zenab placed an oversized question mark after "cod" on her grocery list. What else? she thought, vigorously chewing the end of the pencil, her attention wandering to the television screen again. A segment about Jerusalem was now being aired. The handsome, roving reporter, unchanged in his appearance, disconnected still from his surroundings, was speaking in a crisp accent that wasn't anything resembling what she heard on the streets in New York or Westville. "Jerusalem," he was proclaiming, "named Yeroshalayim by the Jews and Bayt-al-Muqadas by the Muslims, is a city which the Muslims want as much as the Jews and Christians do."

Jewish pilgrims stood in grave postures at the Wailing Wall, called the Wall of Suleiman by the Arabs, Zenab remembered from her high school history book. Suddenly she felt guilty for not saying her prayers regularly and not having read the Koran in what was surely a very long time. If Sakina Phupi discovered she had been so remiss she'd tsk, tsk and shaking her head bemoan the lack of faith among those who had wandered away from home. Just then the muezzin's call to prayer, the azaan, arose and rang like a siren song, insinuating its way into the murmuring of Hebrew prayer and the hubbub of the bazaars. Poor King Hussein. So debonair, so patient. An unhappy monarch who had let Jerusalem slip through his hands.

"O Fab, we're glad/ There's lemon-freshened borax in you!" She remembered she was out of laundry detergent and jotted down "detergent-Fab" on the list that was expanding rapidly. But why not consult the Koran anyway? That was the spring of Islamic law, the source.

She leafed through the Pickthall translation. "The Cow: 2:168. Believers, eat of the wholesome things with which we have provided you . . . He has forbidden you carrion, blood, and the flesh of the swine; also any flesh that is consecrated other than in the name of Allah."

So, the issue was no issue at all. The commandment was clear-cut.

But will Sakina Phupi accede to such argument? No. We're all creatures of custom and habit.

At that moment Zenab envied the women in Lahore who didn't have to torment themselves with such absurd doubts when preparing a feast for an aunt. Their concern would be with the menu, with having enough sugar and milk for kheer, with getting to the market early so that the best portions of mutton or beef could be had, with finding a plump chicken at a reasonable price, and securing enough ice for drinking water. How her cousin Zenab would laugh if she were to see her now. How she would snicker if she knew that Zenab's dinner party was preceded by scholarly research on the matter of halal meat. Zenab blushed at her own foolishness. But Zenab wasn't around to observe her in her moment of weakness. She was alone, and Haider, her son, was too young to know anything.

She browsed through the paperback Koran. On page 357 she read: "Women shall have rights similar to those exercised against men, although men have a status above women. Allah is mighty and wise." I should ask Wazira, she thought. Why hadn't she thought of Wazira before?

Wazira knew most things there were to know. She and her husband, a second-year resident, had been in the United States a little longer than Zenab and Ali and some of the others. Often Zenab had heard Kaneez with the hurried laugh and happy demeanor, announce that when in trouble, ask Wazira. As a matter of fact, Kaneez, had developed quite a distinctive style of her own. A more youthful style, joyfully reckless. Already adept at keeping a close watch on fabric sales and where to buy the best 220-volt appliances at bargain prices for taking back to Pakistan as gifts, she was also keeping a sharp eye on eligible young women who might be suitable for Pakistani bachelors at Grasslands Hospital.

However, Wazira wasn't home, which didn't surprise Zenab at all. She was rarely to be found at home. After all, how could she know so much if she didn't window-shop regularly and hunt for bargains early in the day, before shoppers crowded the stores looking for discounts? Zenab decided to try Kaneez instead and dialed her number. After a few rings Kaneez's sluggish "Hallo" greeted her. Since she didn't have any children, there was a silent agreement among the women that she be allowed to sleep late. Zenab hurriedly apologized for having woken her.

"Don't be silly," Kaneez murmured sleepily. "I was awake, just lying down." For a whole minute she engaged Zenab in a conversation about the fabric sale at Singer's. "Don't forget the dollar-a-yard table at the back of the shop," she advised wisely, her voice clear and sharp. She was fully awake now.

"No, I won't," Zenab assented in haste.

Who cares about the fabric when there are such portentous issues at hand, and anyway, I've already done my fabric shopping for the month. Now, how to do this.

"By the way, Kaneez, is there any halal meat available around here?" Zenab finally asked, forcing a casual tone, aware that by asking she had condemned herself; surely her ignorance would now be evident to all, she thought gloomily.

"Halal? Are you joking? Of course not." Kaneez spoke with such vigor Zenab realized she had indeed made herself look foolish.

She continued energetically. "We always get ours from New York. Are you out?"

"Yes," Zenab said bleakly, playing with her wedding band. Why stop now? "And I need some desperately. We're having company on Sunday and there's no time to go to New York."

Will she offer some of hers? Perhaps if I ask. I wish she offers. A half a pound would do.

"What about kosher?" Kaneez's voice rang with authority.

"Kosher?" Zenab queried inanely. The word had a familiar ring, like the name of an acquaintance whose face doesn't register right away.

Oh my God! Yes! I've seen it on hot dog labels at Grand Union. Jewish, surely. But what does Kaneez mean?

Afraid of exposing her ignorance further and fully, Zenab didn't elaborate her question. Kaneez loved to talk, so she let her.

"Yes, kosher chicken and kosher turkey and even kosher hot dogs," Kaneez went on. She showed no evidence of being disturbed by Zenab's perplexity on the matter of kosher. "You see, all their meat is prepared just like ours. They recite God's name before slaughtering the animal and bleed the animal afterward."

They? Zenab winced at her own stupidity.

"Anyway, you see, what's kosher is okay for us." Kaneez spoke with greater authority than before. Zenab could picture her at the other end, her small beady eyes shining, her face flushed, the expression on it triumphant with the knowledge that she had offered valuable advice, that she could now move closer to Wazira's league.

"Does Wazira use kosher too?" Zenab asked cautiously.

I have to be sure. Know it all. What if Sakina Phupi decides to crossexamine me?

"Of course, Zenab, we all do when there's an emergency."

All? Ohhh . . .

"Especially in the winter. You see, it's difficult to make frequent trips to the City when the weather's so bad, you know. Thank God for the Jews."

"Yes," Zenab mumbled.

"Pathmark always has a good supply." Not one to give up easily, Kaneez rapidly volunteered more information.

"Oh."

Should I put my trust wholly in Kaneez's word? After all, she's only a fledgling disciple. And isn't a Jewish prayer different from a Muslim prayer?

Chamber's Twentieth Century Dictionary had traveled with Zenab from Pakistan, one of the few books she had brought with her. Inside, on the first blank page was her brother's name, below hers, while her sister's girlish flourish lurched precariously immediately beneath his. The pages of the dictionary, which had belonged to her father, were sere, curling at the edges, and brittle. Gingerly she worked on the top right corner of each page until she had it secure between her forefinger and thumb. Then she lifted it slowly, with care. Twice she went through J and twice, arriving at I, missed K. Finally she wet a finger, slowly leafed this time, found "junk" and, running a finger down, came to "kosher" in the column on the left. Right under Koran. It said: "Pure, clean according to the Jewish ordinances—as of meat killed and prepared by Jews. [Hebrew, from yashar, to be right]."

Crossing out "cod" on her grocery list, Zenab wrote down "kosher chicken—Pathmark" instead.

The segment on fighting in the Middle East was winding down. A mist had settled over Jerusalem. The prayer shawls and abas appeared as dabs of white paint on a dark canvas. The handsome, roving reporter was nowhere in sight. Zenab switched the channel to PBS so that Haider, who was now awake and whimpering sullenly, could watch *Sesame Street*.

The rest of the day dragged. At twelve Zenab watched Hitchcock's *To Catch a Thief*, perhaps for the third time in two months, and when the baby dozed off around two, she too stretched out next to him and fell asleep. In a dream she saw that she and Sakina Phupi were walking about anxiously, lost in an Arab village, looking for a place to buy oregano. In the dream she led her aunt by her arm through a maze of dust-ridden streets white with torrid sunshine, encountering on her way her son who ran from her as if she were a stranger. When she woke up she was sweating and her throat was dry. Just as she was about to get up for a drink of water she heard Ali's key turn in the front door.

Breathless with excitement, she ran to the door. No sooner had Ali stepped into the foyer than she said, holding the door wide open for her husband, "Ali, our troubles are over. Thank God for the Jews!"

Skeena

The air conditioner has been shut off so that the overtaxed insides of the belabored machine can have some rest. The servants are about, straightening bed sheets, vigorously dusting furniture, putting away magazines, stacking up books left from last night's reading on Abbi's bedside table. For the next hour the house will be in a state of systematic disarray while Ramzan, the houseboy, moves bulky upholstered sofas in the drawing room, also chairs, rattan murahs and end tables in order to reach the hard-to-get-to corners. When the floors are swept with long-haired, swishing jharus, and the rugs are thwacked and brushed, small whirling clouds of dust will rise to thicken the air, and Zenab, protecting her just-washed wet hair with her dupatta, will dodge the servants and the furniture to find a place where she can sit down and read.

The new house is too large. It was built for children coming home on weekends, for grandchildren frequently darting and scooting about noisily in the long veranda, for long, tea-sipping evenings of chats after dinner. The children and the grandchildren are in the United States. They come once a year, sometimes not even that. But the empty spaces remain and must be cleaned. Four spacious bedrooms are hugged on the inside by an oversized circular veranda into which a door from every room opens, on the outside, by a lawn that begins with bougainvillea whose thin, contorted trunks are entwined in desperate embraces, their red and purple flowers forming a canopy of color over the front door. At the farthest end of the lawn are rose bushes, jasmine shrubs, and thick-leafed rubber plants. Along the driveway, bordering the front lawn, stand tall magnolias with white flowers as large and graceful as water lilies. In the back of the house, near the servant quarters, is a vegetable garden where Zenab's mother grows okra, coriander, sharp, bitter karela, and long-tendrilled loki. Zenab can feel the taste of cooked karelas in her mouth when she prepares the small, tight green gourds in her own kitchen in Connecticut, but something eludes her and she's disappointed with the way the karelas turn out in her recipe.

Since breakfast Zenab has been in search of a room. Ammi is intent on keeping track of Ramzan and his female companion as the cleaning odyssey swings into motion. Haider, four and undaunted by the intense July heat, happily straddled on his shiny red tricycle, pedals fiercely on the uneven surface of the brick driveway. As for the visitors, restless from the heat and anticipating tall glasses of orange or mango squash as soon as they come in, they will not make an appearance until after eleven. Zenab is forced to seek her own company.

Rising and falling dust screens, the constant high-pitched chatter of the young woman who has been newly hired to mop floors, interspersed with Ammi's "Hurry, don't dawdle," accompanies Zenab as she moves from one place to the next. Finally she finds herself in her father's study. It's a small, secluded antechamber attached to her parents' bedroom, its windows opening out on her mother's vegetable garden. Abbi has left for the office, but the fragrance of his newest after-shave, Aramis this year perhaps, a gift from her brother in New Jersey, hangs thickly in the dense atmosphere of the room.

The tall windows behind heavy cotton draperies remain shut and the draperies haven't been pulled aside as yet. It's dark in the study, close. Across from the windows the dark mahogany bookcases take up an entire wall. Wide-shelved and bent forward from the weight of the books, they seem to wear postures of longing and wonderment. Collections of Persian poetry—Hafiz, Saadi, and Khusrau—the Urdu poets Mir, Hali, Sauda, Wali, Dagh, Ghalib and Iqbal, Faiz, also Faraz, the poet in exile, and innumerable others, are stacked together tightly, spine to spine, aging silently.

Ham vahaan hein jahan se hamko bhi
Kuch hamari khabar nahin aati

I am at a place from where
I receive no tidings of myself.

Turning the ceiling fan on to full speed, Zenab watches it slowly come to life, its narrow blades lazily hacking away at the layer of thick, sultry air that has stood motionless all night. As the first wave of hot air slaps her face she gasps, but slowly the intensity wears off. She drops herself into a cane chair whose long, narrow arms curl inward like clenched fists, and opens her book.

To read in summer is to shut out the heat, to diminish it, or at least you think that is what's happening. Ignoring the slowly inching droplets of sweat that gather behind the ears or at the roots of your hair and feel like crawling ants, you will try, stubbornly to read on. Zenab has brought with her Volume I of *Remembrance of Things Past* in the hope of finally delving into a work that had stood on her bookshelf in Connecticut for nearly two years, neglected, formidable. On the plane she read one chapter. Since her arrival in Lahore the book has remained untouched, until this morning, gathering dust that is diligently wiped by Ramzan when he dusts other things in her room.

. . . the path he is taking will be engraved in his memory by the excitement induced by strange surroundings, by unaccustomed activities, by the conversation he has had and the farewells exchanged beneath an unfamiliar lamp, still echoing in his ears amid the silence of the night, by the imminent joy of going home.

31

A muted shuffle behind her tugs at her attention. It's the young cleaning woman, Ammi's newest employee. She stands in the doorway of the study with one hand placed loosely on her hip, the other clutching a large, gray rag. Before Zenab can open her mouth to protest, she deposits the wet, sagging cloth on the floor, and then, while Zenab watches helplessly, she squats, her knees drawn up to the level of her chin, and begins mopping with great force and determination. Zenab decides not to relinquish her place. Ramzan is nowhere in sight. She can prop her feet on the chair when the woman comes around to where she's sitting, she will continue to read.

Half sprawled on the floor, the upper part of her thin, bony body stretching and retreating alternately in a slow caterpillar-like movement, the young woman pushes, prods, and heaves the sodden rag. Soon she's out of breath. The rag changes tint rapidly, turning from a dull grey to a dark brown while Zenab is watching. On the woman's slender wrists, green and red glass bangles strike against each other, jingling rhythmically as her hands maneuver the mop. Zenab shuts her book; her attention has been deflected, but more than that, the woman's complete dedication to lifting dust from every corner of the room seems to overshadow the narrator's nostalgic lament.

She can't be more than twenty-seven or twenty-eight. Her complexion glistens like a newly polished copper pot and a pair of dark, close-set eyes catch the light from the ceiling lamp and gleam like black marbles when she lifts her face to glance at Zenab. Her hair, straggly and knotted, is bound with a piece of yellow rag, while frizzled wispy strands, escaping from both sides, swing carelessly on either side of her face. Sometimes, using a wet, grubby hand, she absently twists the strands behind her ears.

Zenab's probing look has made her self-conscious. She looks up and smiles, her full, dark lips moving upward slightly. Then, without warning, she lets go of the rag, which plops noisily onto the floor, and her arms draped over her knees, her skinny, thickly veined hands dangling over them, she stares ahead in Zenab's direction. It is only after a few minutes pass that Zenab realizes it's her footwear and not her person to which the woman's attention is riveted.

"What's your name?" Zenab asks.

"Skeena, bibi," she answers, grinning broadly this time, revealing, uneven, yellowed teeth. And with that she rises from the floor, walks over to where Zenab is sitting and plunks herself close to the chair, her eyes still focused on the shoes.

Zenab bends down to examine the object of Skeena's scrutiny. It's an old pair of sandals, narrow dark blue and green straps crisscrossing to form a mesh, a sling back with a wooden platform heel thinned from wear.

"These are nice shoes," Skeena says finally, pointing to the sandals. Then, "You will take them back to Amreeka with you?" she asks, her eyes lifted to Zenab's.

"Do you want them? I won't take them back if you want them." Zenab fingers the straps. "Will they fit?"

"Yes, yes bibi, look." The young woman extends a thin, bony foot, the sole orange with henna, and nods in satisfaction. "You'll leave them for me when you go?"

Zenab nods. But before she can say more, Skeena stoops, picks up the besmirched rag from the floor and leaves the room as quietly as she had come.

Skeena's husband is a bricklayer. For more than a year he has been working on the construction of a house down the street, less than half a mile from Zenab's parents' new home. Caretaker as well, he has lodgings in the lot's compound, a small room thatched with mud and straw, a square opening with a sackcloth curtain for a window and a bamboo jalousie where a door should have been. Zenab can see it from the road when she walks in the evening with Ammi. He and his family have come from a village some thirty miles south of the colony, one of several nondescript villages with difficult names that have existed for years on the outskirts of what is now a new and carefully planned township for retired civil servants and the well-to-do.

They are nomads, these bronze-faced farmers who have left their ancestral villages and wide, open tilling fields to seek employment and disappear into the tightly knit streets of rapacious cities. Zenab sees them every year when she's here, and each time there seem to be more and more of them. When the house under construction is complete, Skeena's husband will move on to another site, with his wife and children if he has a room in the compound, or he will send Skeena and her baby to live with his mother in the village.

Zenab chats often with Skeena in the days following their first meeting. Between rounds of sweeping, mopping and washing, Skeena takes short breaks and the two women talk as if they were old friends. Zenab has told her about snow in Connecticut, about the hilly roads that surround her house, the season called fall, when dying leaves sputter in riotous color, and the work she must do herself, without any help. Skeena listens wide eyed and feels sorry for the poor bibi who has to dip her hands in the toilet to clean it. "Take me with you," she says laughingly.

One afternoon while Zenab is alternately flipping through *Film Times* and using it to fan herself during a muggy, sticky period of load-shedding, Skeena shares her gravest secret with her. Haider, exhausted from his frenetic morning play in the yard outside, is asleep and, prevented by the heat from returning to Proust or anything of equal substance, Zenab is sprawled in an easy chair with the film magazine. Skeena, who had been mopping when the electricity went off and the fan came to a dead halt, is sitting back, her legs straightened in front of her. She holds the edges of her brightly flowered shirt between the tips of her fingers, flaps it back and forth for air, and says, "I'm saving money to buy a sewing machine."

Zenab looks up from a picture of Sridevi. "India's hottest Bollywood star," the photo caption proclaims.

"Really?" she asks, "a sewing machine? Do you like to sew?"

"Yes, and when I have the machine I will stitch for all the ladies in the bungalows, I won't be cleaning any more." Skeena drops her shirtfront and leans forward. "I have hundred rupees already," she rolls her dark, deep-set eyes and whispers conspiratorially.

"But that's wonderful Skeena, how did you do it?" Excitedly

Zenab thinks she can give Skeena another fifty before she leaves. In her mind rise images of Skeena the successful seamstress, a woman who would no longer have to mop and clean and listen to taunts from the likes of Ramzan. And then she could even stitch all of Zenab's clothes during her annual visits to Lahore.

"I've been saving for a year, bibi, I hide it from my husband, I've stitched it into my quilt. He'll never find it." She chuckles, pulling up a corner of her dupatta to her face to hide her smile. Her ten-month-old daughter wakes up and Skeena gathers her up in her lap. She's a sickly child who sleeps fitfully on a dirty towel behind a sofa or a chair while Skeena works. Sometimes the infant wakes up and begins whimpering in a raw, gasping voice. Taking her in her lap, Skeena sits cross-legged behind one of the large sofas in the drawing room, pulls up her kameez and nurses her daughter until she returns to sleep.

"But Skeena, why do you hide the money from your husband?" Zenab asks, suddenly remembering how often she has hidden a pair of new shoes from her husband, or a handbag, or a new skirt.

"Ai hai bibi, you are too much. If he finds out, he'll take it all from me. He wants a horse for his own tonga, he's been talking about his own tonga for a long time, but bibi, am I mad? I'll not give him even one penny, no, not even one. I work hard, and I'm getting my machine." She gesticulates wildly with her long-fingered hands as she speaks. Streams of sweat speed down the sides of her face, disappearing into the folds of her faded white cotton dupatta that hangs limply from her shoulders. The baby at her breast starts and begins making loud sucking noises.

"How much is the machine?" Zenab asks, telling herself she could give Sheena a hundred easily. The dollar is fifteen rupees this summer.

"Five hundred rupees, bibi, maybe a little more by the time I have all the money." Skeena's baby is asleep again.

The next morning the rains come. A torrent releases itself from the skies which, all these weeks, had been unrelentingly, cruelly silent.

Quickly the heat slackens its hold on the air, timidly crouching low, close to the earth as wet pushes it downward. There's also a sibilant breeze, moist and fragile, rustling like a melody through summer leafage, a cool touch upon burning cheeks.

Jubilation exists everywhere, in the hearts of grouchy, overworked men and tired women, and in the lithe, quick bodies of half-naked children who dance without restraint in the morning rain. Normal, everyday activities are interrupted. Gurgling thunder rolls in darker clouds across the heavily overcast, smoky gray skies, people break into smiles.

In Zenab's parents' house, too, the cleaning is postponed. After dawdling in the veranda for nearly an hour, watching the downpour as if it were a picture show, Abba finally leaves for work. Zenab stays in the veranda with her mother. Haider, fascinated and invigorated by the deluge, is jumping up and down on the sodden, yellowed summer grass, his arms akimbo, the words from his mouth a garbled rendition of childish rapture.

"Look, look Mom, I'm taking a shower, look, look!"

Zenab waves to him. He is running across the lawn, his clothes already soaked and clinging to his small frame.

"Let's have tea, Ammi," Zenab says, looking at her mother, who seems to be half asleep in her chair, her head fallen to one side, her glasses low on her nose.

"Ramzan," Zenab calls out, but Ramzan doesn't answer; he's washing dishes noisily and perhaps can't hear her.

"He's busy, you go yourself," Ammi mutters, stirring. "Don't burn the milk."

Just as Zenab is getting up from her chair she spots Skeena on the driveway. Running toward the house, her head thrown down in an attempt to avoid getting her face wet, she has one arm extended ineffectually as protection against the rain, while the other lashes at the air as she runs. The breeze momentarily catches her dupatta in a billow.

"There's Skeena," Zenab says with a laugh. "She is punctual."

Zenab goes in to see about tea and on her return to the veranda finds a drenched and disgruntled Skeena wringing her dupatta, muttering invectives under her breath as the water drips from her clothes to form tiny puddles on the veranda floor. Ammi is watching her with an expression of dismay.

"Where's the baby, Skeena?" This is the first time Skeena has been here without the child.

"She's with her father, he's not working today, no work on rainy days." Skeena flings the dupatta about, the filmy blue cotton forming a cloud before her face. When she lowers the covering, Zenab observes a dark, ugly bruise on her left cheek, a reddish purple discoloration that hangs over her skin like an ominous shadow.

"What's that?" Zenab points to her face in alarm.

"He must have hit her, her husband, he must have hit her," Ammi says as if she has expected it, was waiting for it to happen.

Skeena nods, her face lit with her characteristic smile. Her lips turn upward, the movement incongruent against the dark stiffness of the bruise on her cheek.

"Yes, he slapped me, bibi," she says simply, breaking again into a smile as she gathers her wet shirt front in her hands and twists it energetically.

"But Skeena, why? And what's there to smile about?" Zenab feels as if these two women, her mother and Skeena, have a secret they haven't shared with her; they know something she doesn't. For a moment she feels like someone who has failed an exam. Distressed, she glances at her mother for an explanation. Ammi is leaning back in her chair, her eyes closed again, her lips pressed together tightly.

Skeena giggles. "He was angry I was making daal everyday, he wants meat," she tries to explain, waving her hands about as she speaks. "But you see, bibi, meat is ten rupees a seer, how can I cook meat every day?"

"And so he hit you?" Zenab grabs her arm and shakes her.

"Bibi, why do you want to know?" Skeena asks plaintively. Dropping her wet dupatta on the back of a chair, she sits down. Her damp, sticky hair, released from the confines of the yellow rag, is spread on her shoulders, her lean hands are draped fanlike over her bony knees. "He knows I'm hiding the money," she whispers, without waiting for Zenab's reply. "He wants it for his tonga and I'm not giving it to him. It's for my machine and I'm not giving it to anyone." Her voice assumes a solemn tone, the smile leaves her face, a thin furrow creases her forehead and her eyes become clouded, the lights palled by deepening shadows. "It's mine, isn't it?" she says simply.

The three women silently watch the rain first diminish, then stop. A hush falls over the surrounding landscape—the lawns, the verandas—and light returns to the sky bringing with it a promise of increased humidity. The gutters putter weakly, making feeble noises, poor imitations of the deafening torrent raging only moments ago. Zenab and her mother leave the veranda to go inside. Skeena begins mopping up the wet muddy veranda floor.

Skeena doesn't mention the money again. But a week later her husband comes to the house asking to see Amma. It's just after dinner. Ramzan is clanking pots in the sink, Abbi has taken Haider for a ride in the car, and Zenab is on the front lawn with Ammi. It's past nine, but some light still lingers, struggling to hold its own against the encroaching darkness. The pedestal fan whirs noisily, the crickets, euphoric from the morning's rain, make crazed music, and the frogs, anxious not to be left behind, croak vociferously. The evening is filled with the sounds of summer, the air redolent with summer scents, the opulent fragrance of jasmine and raat ki rani, the tantalizing aroma of wet earth, the occasional whiff of ginger, coriander and turmeric drifting from the kitchen.

Skeena's husband comes with Ramzan. The man has a quiet face, deeply lined, too deeply lined for a man his age, and his eyes are lowered in deference to Zenab and her mother, not harsh or brazen. Zenab can't picture him as a wife beater. Tall and well built, his skin ruddy like a copper pot from constant exposure to the sun, he stands passively next to Ammi's chair after an initial exchange of salutations and politely murmurs answers to her questions about the progress of the house he's working on. Then, after a moment's silence he says, in a pleading, unhappy tone, "Bibi, please let Skeena go."

He seems to hunch forward as he speaks and looks, not at the two women, but past them, at the darkness of the shrubbery behind them.

"What has happened? Has something happened?" Ammi sits up and asks sharply.

"Nothing has happened, bibi, but she shouldn't be working for other people." His voice, hoarse, uneven, clotted with emotion, betrays his desperation. "There's enough work at home, there's the girl, and she . . . she brings me shame by working in other people's homes. There's no need, she's not starving." He shifts his weight from one foot to the other, and with his right hand he slowly rubs the back of his neck.

"I'll talk to her when she comes tomorrow, but she'll have to finish this month with us, she took an advance from me. Do you understand?" Ammi looks at him sharply.

"Yes, bibi." The man's words are barely audible.

"But you shouldn't have raised your hand to her. Why did you do that?"

He recoils from her accusing gaze. "She hides money from me, bibi," he mutters in an agitated tone. "She doesn't spend it on food, she has this stupid idea she's going to buy a machine and start a tailoring business. Why? I must have a tonga. Is my tonga more important or her machine? And if I don't give her the money, she steals it from me." He's rubbing his neck again, while with his other hand, which is broad palmed and rough skinned, he smoothens out the front of his long, white cotton shirt.

"I'll talk to her tomorrow," Ammi says, leaning back in her chair before he turns to leave.

Skeena doesn't come to work the next day, or the day after that. Following some voluntary investigation on Ramzan's part, it becomes known that she has gone to the village to be with her sick mother. There seems no point in waiting for her. Ramzan is instructed to look for a new cleaning woman.

"But we must try and find out if she's coming back," Zenab protests when Ramzan starts bringing in other women.

Ramzan tries to hide his irritation. "Bibi, you don't know anything. She's not an honest person. I tell you, you should look properly in your room, you should see she hasn't taken anything." He exhibits exaggerated concern as he ushers in new candidates for the cleaning job.

"No, no, Ramzan," Zenab admonishes indignantly "she wasn't that sort of a person. You shouldn't say such things about her."

But why did she leave so suddenly? Zenab feels uneasy. Has she allowed herself to be drawn into a friendship with this woman? Or is it that she wanted to see her face when she gave her the money for the machine and then the sandals. Yes, the sandals. Why, she has almost forgotten the sandals.

Later Zenab looks for the sandals. They've disappeared. She searches everywhere; in the almirahs, behind furniture, in her father's study where she has spent so much time, in the lawn where she and her mother sit together in the evenings. There's no sign of the shoes anywhere. Ramzan joins the search, muttering as he drags sofas and chairs away from the walls, "I say, bibi, she's taken them. You know she wanted them, so she stole them. I knew from the beginning she wasn't to be trusted." He cannot disguise his sense of victory.

Why did she not ask for them? Zenab abandons her search. The shoes are nothing, she thinks. But why is she feeling dispirited? She remembers that Skeena had been hiding money from her husband, and perhaps other things as well. Could she have taken the shoes because she couldn't wait? What else has she taken? Zenab wonders if she should go through the drawer where she keeps her jewelry. No, it must be the shoes only, she hastens to assure herself. Because they were there, discarded, and, unable to fend off temptation, Skeena had taken them.

In the ensuing weeks a new cleaning girl begins work at her mother's house and Zenab tries not to think about Skeena and the shoes. One morning, while she's going through some books on the shelves in her father's study, she hears Ramzan and the cleaning girl arguing loudly in the corridor. The girl's high-pitched voice rises and falls in protestation followed by Ramzan's overheated protests. Then Ammi's irate "Why are you making so much noise?" rings out.

Zenab comes out to find all three standing in a group in the corridor outside her bedroom. Ramzan's face is flushed. He is obviously agitated. The new cleaning girl has a long jharu in her hand that she extends outward as if it were a sword. Ammi's brow is wrinkled in consternation. Zenab joins them.

On the floor, before them, like some dead animal, covered with layers of dust and lint, the leather straps curled and twisted with heat, and faded beyond recognition, sit the lost sandals.

"I just made a long sweep under the bed with my jharu, bibi, and I felt something next to the wall. It was your shoes, hiding in the corner." A broad triumphant grin maps the young girl's face as she looks excitedly at Zenab.

Ramzan says gruffly, "She was in your room alone, bibi, I've told her never to go in any of the rooms unless I'm with her." Furiously waving a hand he acts as if he hasn't heard what the girl is saying. He avoids Zenab's gaze.

"Now stop, both of you," Ammi says angrily, "the shoes have been found and that's all that matters."

Speechless, Zenab feels as if she's a child caught in a lie. How frail her trust has been, how easily broken. Awkwardly she gropes for some words about the discovery that has caused such excitement. She doesn't know what to say. It's as if she has intruded into a happenstance in which she has no part. How little she knows these people, she realizes, Ramzan, Ammi, Skeena, or even her father who waits for the grandchild who will read Urdu and inherit his books. What illusions she has created for herself during her short visit. As if by some magic, the dusty, crumpled sandals have appeared to shatter that illusion. Zenab wishes the shoes had lain under the bed in silence for a while longer, until she had left this place.

"Shall I clean them, bibi?" the cleaning girl asks, squatting on the floor, the jharu abandoned, her hands lovingly fondling the shoes.

"Do you still want them, bibi?"

"No, no, of course you can take them," Zenab mumbles absently.

It is Zenab's last evening in Lahore. She and Haider are walking. The colony is shrouded in dark and brooding silence. The hour is late, past nine, and the only sounds Zenab hears are the clitter-clatter of her son's Bata sandals on the gravel as he skips and hops a few feet ahead of her, also the occasional barking of a stray dog somewhere in the shadow of night, and sometimes the honking of an automobile on the main road.

Zenab and her son are only a few yards from her parents' house when she spots Skeena. The child hangs limply, sluggishly, on her hip, and in the half darkness, both mother and child seem to be a part of the fogginess that sits unmoving outside the wrought iron gate. She stirs silently as Zenab approaches, but she doesn't come forward.

"Where have you been, Skeena?" Zenab asks anxiously as she comes closer. Then, remembering how she has misjudged her, she feels blood rise to her face. "Are you all right?" she asks, fighting the awkwardness in her tone.

Skeena's voice is a hoarse whisper. "I had to go to the village, bibi." Her voice is hollow, without inflection, flat and empty like the expression on her face. "My mother was sick," she adds, looking away, into the darkness.

"You should have told us you were leaving," Zenab begins, intending to be firm, but she doesn't finish. Skeena turns to look at her and Zenab sees her face clearly for the first time as the light from the boxed lamp on the gate illuminates it.

Skeena's eyes are dark and swollen. There are long blue-green and purple shadows along her left cheek, like a carefully designed tattoo etched permanently into the skin.

"Ya Allah! What happened, Skeena?" Shocked, Zenab extends a hand toward the young woman.

"My man took away the money, bibi, he bought a horse for his tonga," Skeena says simply.

Her eyes fill with tears, she shifts uneasily on her feet and sniffles.

Zenab doesn't know what to say to her. Words fail her. She wants to comfort Skeena, but the silence grows ponderous on her tongue and she says nothing.

Lifting a corner of her dupatta, Skeena wipes her nose with it.

"Let's go, Mom," Haider tugs at his mother's kameez.

Skeena pushes her baby higher up on her hip. The look on her face challenges Zenab's faltering gaze.

"Bibi, can you give me the shoes now?" she asks, her dark eyes suddenly bright with the eager light of her question.

The Poor Boys . . .

"**W**ait till I tell you this," Halima Khala says in a conspiratorial tone, leaning her heavy bulk toward me as she speaks, her eyes narrowed and glinting fiercely, her forehead creased.

A story then. The vegetables—squash, tough-skinned bell peppers, dark green, wrinkled leafy spinach, and squat tubular green beans—will have to wait in the colander a while longer. Halima Khala will be hurt if I don't give her all my attention.

This is my aunt's first visit to the United States. In the beginning she had stubbornly fought the idea of travelling across what she liked to refer to as "the seven seas," inventing excuses that were like water through a sieve, feigning malaria as a last resort. Even her husband failed to coerce her.

"She says her heart's all dried up and there's no feeling in her left leg," her son Fahim told me once after he received another excuse from her. "And she'll have a heart attack on the plane, she says," he added in frustration.

Finally, after some underhanded, devious plotting in which his father was commissioned to play a surreptitious role, Fahim sent her a roundtrip PIA ticket, which he should have done in the first place, and she had no choice but to make the dreaded crossing across the seven seas. "I didn't want to come, but I couldn't throw away my son's hard-earned money, now, could I? He's not picking money from trees, is he?" She explains her presence earnestly to everyone she meets.

Somewhat breathless from the walk up the stairs to our living room, she now sits on the sofa stiffly, one plump arm crossed over the other, a worried look mapped across her face, as if she has forgotten something important, which she is struggling to remember. Two thick gold bangles fit snugly around one puffy wrist, a tiny white bead in her nose glimmers like a star, and a pair of gold filigreed earrings dig deep into flattened, papery earlobes. Her gray hair, thin and flat on her head like a cap, is streaked orange with henna. When she talks, she plays absently with her bracelets, turning them round and round, occasionally lowering her eyes to observe them, then looking up again with a sigh.

She has brought me a gift.

"Open it, Zenab," she encourages with a portly smile, pointing to the shalwar-kameez suit in my lap.

Fine, lacy lawn with white embroidery, the dupatta a foamy muslin that reminds me of the days when I was a teenager in high school and wore nothing but muslin during the long hundred-degree summers.

Like wings, the white muslin flew in the sun-baked summer breeze.

"It's the latest style," Halima Khala says, "and all the young girls are wearing it in Lahore. You like it, don't you?"

"Yes, yes I like it very much Khala, it's beautiful, just the thing for summer." I give the suit in my lap an approving pat and thank her.

Yes, yes, tell me more, I plead, impatient with pauses.

"Zenab, you're like my daughter," she explains. "I wanted to get you more things, bangles, some silver jewelry, but there was such a rush before I left, and your uncle kept insisting I shouldn't have too much baggage, and Fahim said on the phone, 'Amma, don't bring too many suitcases.' Boys, such a fuss they make sometimes."

45

She glances in the direction of the deck where Ali and my cousin are hunched over the grill trying to bring the charcoal brickets to life.

"Zeni child, what are those two doing in the heat?" she asks suspiciously after a moment's silence.

"Oh, they're going to roast chicken on the grill, Khala," I offer hastily, "like we used to roast it on live coals sometimes in Lahore when you came to visit? You'll like it."

Later, as I propel her by the elbow toward the kitchen where vegetables are not the only thing waiting to get done, she again peers anxiously at the men, this time through the screen door.

"They are cooking?" she asks with some displeasure. "Why are they cooking?"

"Don't worry, Halima Khala, they're just going to watch as the chicken cooks, you know, so it doesn't burn." I can see she would have liked us to be out on the porch and Ali and Fahim in here, sprawled on the sofas in the living room, puffing on their cigarettes and discussing Prime Minister Benazir's Bhutto's latest fiasco.

"They'll ruin it, what do they know about chicken?" She shakes her head despondently.

While I'm washing a head of Boston lettuce, Halima Khala, seated at the kitchen table now, sighs deeply a number of times. Something is troubling her and it isn't just that the men are cooking. I turn to look at her, and catching my eyes, she leans forward and immediately says, "Wait till I tell you this."

The salad must stay. I wash my hands and sit down across from my aunt. "What happened, Khala?" I ask. Outside, my husband and Fahim have started talking loudly, in overheated tones, perhaps forgetting the grill altogether.

Halima Khala is slumped in her chair. Her hands are stretched out in her lap, palms down, her bracelets still. And she's not aware that her dupatta has slipped from her head and lies huddled over her shoulders like an abbot's fallen cowl. Sunlight from our kitchen window dances with wild abandon on the white wall behind her, spilling over every now and then over her chiffon dupatta in jumbled patterns.

The Poor Boys . . .

"Khala, what is it?" She hasn't eaten pork by accident, has she? Poor woman, what grief! My interest piqued, I move to the edge of my seat.

"Girl, I could not believe it. What has happened? I'm afraid for my son, and you should start worrying about your sons as well."

Not pork then. Has she accidentally run into a Pakistani girl in a bathing suit? Her legs bare, the fullness of her chest exposed? Fahim had been planning to take her to the beach. Or perhaps a neighbor's young daughter in tight jeans and a bosom-hugging T-shirt. There are a lot of Pakistanis in Fahim's apartment building in Edison, New Jersey. She may even have seen men and women in a state of half-dress kissing each other in a soap opera on television—no, worse still, convulsing nearly all naked under coverlets.

Just then, before Halima Khala can bring herself to say another word, Kasim walks into the kitchen and heads straight for the refrigerator. Silently she follows him with her gaze, a quick, expectant smile frozen on her lips.

I shake my son's arm impatiently. "Kas, Halima Khala is here, aren't you going to say salaamaleikum?" Children can disappoint you in ways you have never imagined.

"Oh . . . salaam . . . uh . . . aleikum," the boy mumbles, color rising to his face instantly, his hand nervously brushing the edge of the refrigerator door.

"Waleikumassalaam!" Halima Khala's face relaxes into a large, happy grin and she extends her arms out to him. He glances at me helplessly, then at her arms, moves away from the refrigerator and gradually inches forward. She grasps his arm and pulls him to her, his lanky arms crossed like sticks beneath her embrace. She kisses his forehead. "How he has grown, Zenab, he was just a baby when you were in Lahore last time." She kisses him again, this time on his cheek. "Where was he?" she asks, letting him go.

"At a game." I wonder if Khala will tell everyone in Lahore my son had to be told to offer proper salutations. "Ten years old, and still has no idea how to greet his elders." Perhaps she'll forget, perhaps she'll have other, more exciting tales to tell.

The story.

What? What? The children wait eagerly. So the princess left her home in the sea to marry the prince who lived on land. What then?

"Khala, so what happened?" I press. The men are hunched over the grill again, this time in silent concentration.

"Do you know Arif?" Halima Khala begins. "Fahim's friend who was with him in college? He's a doctor and he got married last December?"

"Yes, I've met him once, he came with Fahim for lunch one weekend, but that was before he was married. What is his wife like?"

"Now listen, Zenab, forget what she's like. They invited us for dinner."

O God! The girl didn't cook halal meat—the fool! But everyone knows about halal meat and where to get it; the Diaspora is firmly in place.

Halima Khala continues. "I'm not old fashioned, I know the world has advanced, I'm not easily shocked." She lifts a hand self-assuredly.

It isn't the meat then.

"But I tell you, child, there are some things we old people should never see. Nadira, that's her name, cooked a good meal for us. I can't say she doesn't know how to cook and the more's the pity."

What? What? The sea princess promised she would come back because on land her life would diminish, she would stifle.

Like an eager child I want Halima Khala to get to the pith of the story, to the final stab.

"Acha, acha . . ."

"She's a doctor, a children's doctor, pedia-something, Fahim said. Very pretty, long black silky braid, and very fair complexion, and such a nice, pointed nose."

I realize Halima Khala would have liked my hair to be long and in a braid as well. A girl's hair is her adornment, she'd say.

"And what nice china, English I think, a blue and pink design, little flowers, you know, very dainty. And the carrot halwa was so good, Fahim had three helpings and in spite of my diabetes, I took one small second helping."

Kasim is now leaning against the counter, sipping orange juice from a paper cup; a slice of yellow American cheese dangles precariously from his free hand. Like his older brothers, he too likes carrot halwa, and I fry long and hard, thinking all the time of how it looked and smelled and tasted when one bought it, steamingly fragrant with the aroma of cardamom, from a sweet shop in a congested Lahore street. Cadmium orange and flecked with dollops of white khoya.

Halima Khala continues. "But I forgot the halwa soon. You know what she did?"

"What? Did she leave you alone in the living room and go up to her room for a nap?" Many a working woman has done that, to the horror of visiting relatives who have felt abandoned, neglected, tormented by a feeling that they are not people but furniture that can just sit there while the lady of the house disappears for a nap. Why did they come, they often agonize.

"No, no, girl. First she said, 'Let's go to the living room, Auntie,' and then after I sat down she came and plunked herself next to me. What a friendly girl, I thought. Next she asks me if I've been to the stores as yet."

What? What? The princess sees the jinn and knows she is doomed. She must keep her promise, she must leave the prince and return to her world. Forsaking her infant, she must go alone, for the child is of this world and would drown in her watery home.

"This is what happened." Halima Khala fidgets in her chair, pulls at her dupatta and twirls her bangles. She presses her lips together for a few seconds of silence before resuming. "Arif began clearing the table." She raises her eyes and looks at me expectantly. Her eyebrows are lifted, her mouth half open. The ridge on her forehead thickens.

Outside, Ali and Fahim are sitting at some distance from the grill. Probably cursing the opposition leader Nawaz Sharif now, calling him vile names unfit for women's ears. Letting the chicken cook itself. Smoke rises from the charcoal like thick rain clouds gathering for a storm.

"Oh?"

So? So? Did the princess leave without her child?

"Yes." Halima Khala decides to ignore my feeble response. "The whole day the boy works at the hospital, works on weekends as well, and also has calls at night, Fahim told me. And he started picking up dishes and stacking them on the tray as if he were a bearer in a hotel."

"Hmm, did he?" I watch my aunt's face intently.

"And my son had to get up and give him a hand. Did he have a choice?"

I chuckle. "So Fahim had to pick up dishes."

She resumes her story. Leaning back in her chair, she raises a hand and vigorously waves it back and forth. "Well, listen to this, girl. First Arif spilled the water from the jug on the tablecloth, then the greasy spoons slipped from his hands one by one to the carpet, and he couldn't stack the plates one on top of the other properly. Poor boy! And as for her, well, she just sat next to me, oblivious of what the men were doing, and chattered on and on. I've never seen such a chatty new bride. If she had been my daughter-in-law . . . ah."

Sighing, she slumps sideways, the hand that had been waving in the air now fallen limply in her lamp. Her lips are stretched in an expression of grim disappointment.

The smoke from the grill now slinks across the kitchen window in warning. The smell of burning charcoal fills the kitchen thickly. "We're ready," Ali calls out.

Without warning Halima Khala begins again. "And your cousin looking so foolish too. I was afraid he would drop a plate or two and then where would that pretty set be? But Nadira didn't care. I was too distracted to pay attention to what she was saying. Here we were, two women as strong as wrestlers, prattling away about fabric stores while the men first cleared the table and then started making tea! I couldn't stand it. I said, 'Boys, let me help with the tea.' Nadira got up. Maybe she got the hint. But she said, 'Oh Auntie, don't worry, Arif makes very bad tea. I'll make the tea myself.' The poor boy, he works like a slave in his own home and then he's told he makes bad tea. Tell me, Zeni, why must he clear the table like an orderly?" A questioning hand is raised and remains suspended until I speak.

"But Khala, he was home that day, he wasn't working." She hasn't seen him washing the dishes then, or dusting, or mopping the kitchen floor, or sponging the mess around the stove after a meal has been cooked.

"So what if he was. Shouldn't a man rest?"

"Yes, but she works too, you know. And he was only helping, Khala, these days men help their wives." I banter, hoping to mollify her, ignoring the edict, "Don't argue with your elders."

She continues unrelentingly, "Girl, there's man's work and there's woman's work. Your uncle is still taking care of the shop, but even if he weren't, he wouldn't be in the kitchen with me, or in the dining room clearing dishes, now, would he?"

In trying to imagine my uncle in the kitchen I am reminded of the stirring, sappy dramas we used to put on for ourselves as children where I, being the oldest and tallest, would dress up as a man complete with a pencilled mustache, a turban and dhoti. And that wasn't all. I felt like a man.

"It isn't proper that a man clears the table in his own house while his wife chatters away like a parrot. Now tell me, do you make your husband's tea or does he make it himself?"

The story isn't that long, but Halima Khala tells it with such verve and passion I feel as if I have been listening to her for hours. I remember the stories we heard her tell when we were children and she would come to Lahore for a visit: fairies and jinns practicing magic that was as unpredictable as the endings to the stories were predictable, royal tyrants who beheaded people at a whim, long suffering princes who patiently solved abstruse puzzles and put their lives in danger for princesses they had never seen, doomed princesses who had to leave their homes for love and then leave their homes again be-

51

cause their time was up, and the parrot who told all. Khala hasn't lost her touch.

"Tea?" I leave my chair. "Khala, Ali makes such good tea, once you've tasted it you'll never want to drink my tea." I tease my aunt, but she's not smiling.

Her face looks careworn; like corrugated leather, it is mapped with deeply etched lines that seem not to care any more what path they follow. From the kitchen bay window the New England July sun filters through the silver strands in her hair, dips over the foamy white of her dupatta on which little two and three-petaled embroidered flowers appear to be scattered in disarray and, falling across one dark cheek, rests there like a permanent skin discoloration.

The ocean swallowed her. And the pearls are her tears that she sheds as she cried for the child she left on land.

"The poor boys," Halima Khala murmurs as if speaking to herself. With her stubby, gnarled fingers, their tips orange from henna, she reaches to adjust the dupatta over her head. "The poor boys," she says again, looking past me, through the window, at the men outside.

Brave We Are

"**M**om, Ammi," he asks, the little boy Kasim who is my son, who has near-black eyes and whose buck teeth give him a Bugs Bunny look when his mouth is open, as it is now, in query. "What does hybrid mean?"

"Hybrid?" I'm watching the water in the pot very closely; the tiny bubbles quivering restlessly on its surface indicate it's about to come to boil. Poised over the pot, clutching a batch of straw-colored Prince spaghetti, is my hand, suspended, warm from the steam and waiting for the moment when the bubbles will suddenly and turbulently come to life.

I'm not fussy about brands, especially where spaghetti is concerned (it's all pasta, after all), but I wish there was one which would fit snugly at the outset into my largest pot. As things stand now, the strands bend uncomfortably, contort, embroiling themselves in something of a struggle within the confines of the pot once they've been dropped into the boiling water. Some day of course, I will have a pot large enough to accommodate all possible lengths and varieties.

"Yeah, hybrid. Do you know what it means?"

The note of restive insistence in his voice compels me to tear my gaze away from the water. Kasim's face looks darker now than when

he left for school this morning. Perhaps running up the steep driveway with the March wind lashing against his lean nine-year-old
frame has forced the blood to rush to his face. Flushed, his face reminds me he's still only a child, "only ten, just a baby," as my mother
often says when I sometimes take him to task in her presence, arguing
with him as if he were a man behaving like a child.

A new spelling word? Such a difficult word for a fourth-grader.
"Are you studying plants?"

"No, but can you tell me what it means?" Impatient, so impatient,
so like the water that's hissing and tumbling in the pot, demanding
immediate attention. He slides against the kitchen counter and hums,
his fingers beating an indecipherable rhythm on the Formica, his eyes
raised above mine, below mine, behind me, to the window outside
which white, lavender and gray have mingled to become a muddied
brown. Just as he reaches for the cookie jar I quickly throw in the spaghetti.

"Well, that's a hard word. Let me see." Helplessly I watch as he
breaks off a Stella Doro biscuit in his mouth and crumbs disperse in a
steady fall-out, over the counter, on the kitchen tile, some getting
caught in his blue-and-green striped sweater, like flies in a spider's
web. "It's a sort of mixture, a combination of different sorts of
things," I say wisely, with the absolute knowledge that "things" is
susceptible to misinterpretation. I rack my brain for a good example.
If I don't hurry up with one he's going to move away with the notion
that his mother doesn't know what hybrid means.

"You mean if you mix orange juice with lemonade it's going to become hybrid juice?" The idea has proved ticklish, he smiles, crumbs
from the Stella Doro dangling on the sides of his face; they obviously
don't bother him as much as they bother me. I lean forward and rub a
hand around his mouth just as he lunges toward the cookie jar again.
He squirms and recoils at the touch of my ministering hand. Another
biscuit is retrieved. I turn down the heat under the spaghetti to me-
dium and start chopping onions.

Today I'm making spaghetti the way my mother makes it in Lahore, like pulao, the way I used to make it after I got married and was just learning to cook for a husband who had selective tastes in food. That was about the only thing I could make then so I worked hard to embellish and innovate. There, we call it noodles, although it's unmistakably spaghetti, with no tomato sauce or meatballs in or anywhere near it, no cheese either, and no one has heard of mozzarella or romano. The idea of cheese with our recipe would surprise the people in Lahore; even the ones with the most adventurous palates will cringe.

"Well, that too." And why not? My eyes smart from the sharpness of the onions, tears fill my eyes and spill over my cheeks. I turn away from the chopping board. "The word is used when you breed two different kinds of plants or animals, it's called cross-breeding." I sniffle. This gets harder. I know his knowledge of "breeding" is limited and "cross" isn't going to help at all.

"What's cross-whatyoumaycallit?"

An example. One that will put the seal on hybrid forever. So he can boast his mother knows everything.

I wipe my watering eyes with a paper napkin and turn to the onions again. These, chopped thinly, are for the ground beef which will be cooked with small green peas, cubed potatoes and cut-leaf spinach and will be spiced with coriander, garlic, cumin, a touch of turmeric and half-inch long bristly strands of fresh ginger root. I'll throw the beef into the spaghetti when it's done and my husband I alone will eat what I make. My children like spaghetti the way it should be, the way it is, in America.

Moisture runs down my cheeks and my eyes smart. I place the knife down on the chopping board, tear out another sheet from the roll of Bounty towels on my right and rub my eyes and nose with it, my attention driven to the stark, brown limbs of trees outside as I wipe my face. The kitchen window that I now face as I do innumerable times during the day, faithfully reflects the movements of time and seasons of the small town in Connecticut where we live, compelling the spirit to buoyancy or, when the tones on its canvas are achromatous and dark, to melancholy, to sadness. Today, the sun is visible again and the white of the snow is distinguishable from the lavender of the bare, thin, stalky birches, unhealthy because we haven't tended them well. Sharply the sun cuts shadows on the clean, uncluttered snow.

Why does snow in February always remind me of February in Lahore? Incongruent, disparate, the seasons have so little in common. March is spring, grass so thick your foot settles into it, roses that bloom firm, their curves fleshy, the colors like undisturbed paint on an artist's palette, the air timberous, weaving in and out of swishing tree branches with the sar, sar, sar of a string instrument. Why do I turn to Eileen, my cleaning lady, and say, "Eileen do you know it's spring in Lahore?" She looks up from the pot she's scrubbing in the kitchen sink with a good-humored smile. "No kidding? Really?" she asks, as if she didn't already know, as if she hadn't already heard it from me before.

An example, yes. "Now take an apple. A farmer can cross-breed a Macintosh apple with a Golden Yellow and get something which is a little bit like both. That will be a hybrid apple." I look closely at the boy's face for some signs of comprehension.

"You mean the apple's going to have a new name, like Macintosh Yellow?" he asks, his forehead creased thoughtfully.

"Yes." Relieved, I return to the onions, making a mental note to check the spaghetti soon, which, languorously swelled now, will have to be taken off from the stove and drained.

"But what about animals? You said there's crosswhatyoumaycallit in animals too." He sprawls against the counter, up and down, right and left, like a gymnast.

"Yes there is. A cow from one family may be bred with a steer from another family and they'll end up with a calf that's a bit like the two of them." I wash my hands and he skips on the floor, dance like steps, his arms raised.

"But man's an animal too, teacher says. Do people also cross . . . umn . . . breed?"

He's humming again. I know the tune now: "Suzie Q/ Suzie Q/ I love you/ O Suzie Q!" It's from a song on his older brother Haider's tape, a catchy tune, sort of stays with you and you can't stop humming it. Both Haider and my younger son, Asghar, were amused when I showed an interest in the song. What do I know about music, their kind of music? Once, nearly two years ago, I tried to bribe Haider to memorize a ghazal by the poet Ghalib. The greatest Urdu poet of the subcontinent, I said passionately, the most complex. Egged on by the fifty dollars I was offering, he mastered the first verse by listening to a tape of ghazals sung by Mehdi Hasan.

Yeh naa thi hamari qismet ke visal-e-yaar hota
Agar aur jeete rehte yehi intizar hota

It was not fated that I should meet my beloved,
Life will merely prolong the waiting

Then, unable to sustain his interest, despite the now a thirty-dollar a verse rate, Haider abandoned the project.

"The word's are too hard," he complained when I protested, somewhat angrily. "The music's easy, but I can't keep up with the lyrics."

And I would have given him the money too. Actually I had decided to give him all of it after he had moved on to the second verse.

"Does that mean Mary is also hybrid?" Kasim's voice crashes into my thoughts of Suzie Q with a loud boom.

I lower the heat under the spaghetti—so what if it's a bit overdone. The yellow-white strands jump at each other in frantic embraces, hurried, as if there's no time to be lost.

"Mary? What are you talking about?" I know exactly what he's talking about. His vagueness passes through the sieve in my head and comes out as clarity. I fill in any blanks, uncannily, never ceasing to be surprised at the way this peculiar magic works.

"You know, Mary Khan, Dr Khan's daughter? She's in my class Mom, you know her."

Yes, I know Mary well. Her full name is Marium. Her father, Amjad Khan and my husband, Ali, were together in the same medical school in Lahore, they graduated the same year, they completed residencies together at the same hospital in New York, where Amjad met and married Helen, a nurse. Helen is English. She's a few years older than I, very tall, almost a half-inch taller than Amjad, and has sleek, golden hair. We're good friends, Helen and I, and at least once a week we meet for lunch at a restaurant, an activity we decided to call "sampling restaurants for later." Over salmon lasagna or papadi chat and dosa or tandoori chicken she'll tell me how difficult Amjad is when it comes to their children, how upset he is that their son has taken it upon himself to date without his father's consent or approval. I'll shake my head and try to explain that Amjad might have dated her, but like a good Muslim father, he can't accept that his son can have girlfriends. "Wait till Mary is older," I say with my hand on Helen's arm, "the Muslim father in him will drop all his masks." Together we do what most women do quite unabashedly: spend a great deal of time talking about husbands.

When Mary was born Amjad said, "We're going to call her Marium, it's a name everyone knows." Familiar and convenient is what he meant, since it's tri-religious. That doesn't sound right, but if we can say bisexual, surely we can say tri-religious too. Why not? After all Islam, Christianity and Judaism all profess a claim to this name. However, before the child was quite one "Marium" was shortened permanently to "Mary."

Kasim is at the breakfast table now, some of his earlier energy dissipated. A small piece of biscuit lies forlornly before him on the table and he fusses with it slowly, obviously unwilling to pop the last bit in his mouth, content just to play with it.

"You know, her mother's English and her father's Pakistani like Dad, and she's got blue eyes and black hair."

"Yes, she does have lovely blue eyes and they look so pretty with her dark hair." I grapple with something to blunt the sharpness of his next question which I anticipate and I know I cannot repel.

"Well, then she's hybrid too, isn't she?" He's looking straight at me. His eyes are bright with the defiance of someone who knows he's scored a point.

Brave we are, we who answer questions that spill forth artlessly from the mouths of nine-year-old purists, questions that can neither be waved nor dismissed with flippant ambiguity. Vigilant and alert, we must be ready with our answers.

"Technically speaking she is, I mean, wait, you can say she is." I lift a hand and stop him before he says more. "But we don't use the word for people." The firmness in my voice sounds forced. "Beta, don't say anything to her, okay?"

"Why? Is it a swear?"

"No!" I hasten with denial. "Of course not. It's just a word we don't use for people, that's all. Understand?"

"But what do you call them then?" He persists. "Mary's like the apple, isn't she? Isn't she? Her name's Mary Khan, isn't it?"

"Yes, Kas, it is. But there's nothing wrong with that name, a name's a name." Kasim looks contemplative. I know he's saying to himself, Mom doesn't really know, but Mary's a hybrid, she's got blue eyes and black hair.

"She's a person Kasim, not an apple. Anyway, you didn't tell me where you heard that word. Is it on your spelling list for this week?"

"No, Mrs Davis was reading us something about plants in the *Weekly Reader*. It's not homework." He shrugs, abandons the Stella Doro and humming, leaves the kitchen.

"Get to homework now," I call after him, wondering if there's an equivalent of "hybrid" in Urdu, a whole word, not one or two strung together in a phrase to mean the same thing. Offhand I can't think of one.

Without meaning to I throw in some oregano into the boiling spaghetti. I shouldn't have done that. How's oregano going to taste in the company of coriander and cumin? Well, no matter, it's too late anyway.

After I've drained the spaghetti I will take some out for the meat mixture, saving the rest for my children. Then I'll add to our portion, my husband's and mine, the beef and vegetable mixture and turn everything over ever so gently, making sure that the spaghetti isn't squelched. The strands must remain smooth, elusive, separate.

Waiting for the Monsoons

An uneasy awakening guarantees that whatever little coolness had insinuated itself into the night as darkness prevailed, has now vanished. The heat in the room weighs me down like a heavy blanket, forcing me to leave the bed quickly, any desire to linger further dispelled by the appearance of white-hot strips of sunlight along the margins of the curtains where they have strayed from the window casings. Standing next to the window I resist a momentary impulse to lift a corner of the weighty cotton drape and look out; encountered head-on, the livid rays of morning light can make one cringe and fall back, and I'm quite sure there are no clouds as yet. Which means we can't go to see our lot today. That must wait another day, perhaps two, depending on when the monsoons come.

Tea, I think, splashing water on my face from the bathroom tap. Already the water is lukewarm, the flow weak and irregular. As the day progresses and the sun rotates around the water tank on the roof of my parents' new house, finally beating upon it full force around noon, one can be assured of a hot bath, an oddity, one might say, in hundred-degree weather. But one doesn't worry about such oddities when there are streams of sweat to contend with and the stale overpowering odor of perspiration that not even soap and talcum powder seem to quell.

The weather in Lahore has changed. Surely it was never as hot as this when we were children, when we lived in Garhi Shahu in the old four-storey house which rose only a short distance away from the road like an aging fortress. We never talked about the weather then, nor did the adults I think, but these days, seemingly endless summer afternoons are filled with lengthy, lethargic discussions of how the rains have abandoned us, how nothing is as it used to be.

I arrive in the kitchen, which is as large as my oldest son's bedroom in Connecticut, and find Ayesha nursing her ten-month-old daughter, her shirtfront lifted discreetly. Only two years older than me, she is my cousin from my mother's side and has my mother's deep-set eyes and wide forehead.

"Where's Ammi?" I ask, surprised to see Ramzan silently turning omelets in the soot-black frying pan with bent edges, a souvenir from our childhood days, favored more than the five or six Teflon-coated pans I have brought over the years from the US for Ammi. I've never known Ammi to trust anyone with the omelets at breakfast, but then Ramzan has been with her since he was a boy.

"She's outside, with mali," Ayesha says, pulling out a stool for me. Her daughter squirms at her breast, the tiny wet mouth groping for the nipple that has been momentarily lost.

I look out the kitchen window. Ammi's back is to me. She's talking to the gardener who is crouched low, retrieving for her what's ready to be pulled off the branches. There'll be bhindi, called okra where I live, to bring in, also small tight tomatoes tinged with green, so different from the full, pulpous orange-red tomatoes in the fresh-vegetable section in Stop and Shop, so slight in comparison.

"Zenab, did you ever see such beautiful bhindi?" Ammi will ask me, cradling the vegetables in one pale, squat palm while she strokes them with the fingers of the other hand, separating one grooved pod from the other as if she has, spread out on her palm, not just olive-green bhindi, but emeralds.

Ramzan hands me tea and goes to the sink to busy himself with clanking pots. His long white cotton kurta is diagrammed in the back with elongated perspiration stains. He is nearly as tall now as my brother MH with whom he used to fly kites on the roof in the old house when they were both children. Dressed in nothing but loose, knee-length khaki shorts that flapped against their spindly legs, the two boys ran from one end of the veranda to the other with the cord clutched tightly in their hands, the wind in their hair, their faces ruddy from the exertion of the game. This year Ramzan became a father.

"Drink your tea Zenab it's getting cold," Ayesha says. She's here only to see me. With her husband and three children, she lives in a village on the outskirts of Lahore. The village has an unusual name I can never remember and is one of innumerable others that are strewn about in a haphazard way on the boundaries of larger towns and cities. Her husband, Rafique, a tall, thin man who walks with a stoop and has tired eyes, teaches at a boys' school in that village, earning about one thousand rupees a month. It's easy to calculate that it's only forty dollars; the dollar is twenty-five rupees this year.

"Allah! It's so hot!" I pull back the hair from my forehead and neck so I can keep it from touching my face. It flops right back. How foolish that I had cut it so short, that I had forgotten how I would curse myself for not being able to tie it up. Ayesha's baby is staring at me. I lean over to pinch her cheek. The girl pouts, narrows her small, round, coal-black eyes, then hastily burrows her face in her mother's breast.

"Don't you think she's too old to be still nursing?" I ask Ayesha.

"I don't know what to do, she's so spoilt," Ayesha replies, smiling sheepishly. "Now tell me, Zenab, when are you going to build the boundary wall on your plot?" She pulls her shirt down over her breast and covers the child's face with her cotton dupatta to keep off the flies.

I tussle with semantics. "Lot" in the US, "plot" in Pakistan.

"I don't know, Ayesha," I say, feeling uncomfortable that I have to lie. We had bought some land not far from my parents' new house when we thought that soon, very soon, we were to come back and settle in Lahore. In those days making elaborate plans to return was not only a prerequisite of our condition, it was also fashionable, a coffee-table subject that we debated hotly and animatedly at get-togethers. Now my husband and I, like others before us, will only return for visits. Phupi Alima called me a traitor when we brought our decision to the family, and Amma was so angry she couldn't bring herself to speak to me, and Ayesha said, in a pitying tone, "You'll regret this."

But the land remains. An investment, we're told. And we should build a boundary wall like all others who have empty lots, and if we fail to do so the authorities, who know nothing of, and care little about, our dilemma, will confiscate the land. These were the conditions of the sale. I should go and see our lot, though, reexamine its possibilities. Yes, as soon as the clouds come.

"Building a wall isn't cheap, you know," I begin seriously, "and at this time we don't have the money for it. It is a big expense after all." Stretching out my legs, I rest my head against the door of the reddish brown cabinet behind me that still exudes a mildly lingering odor of varnish. "And not one we can't put off."

Ayesha chuckles. "If you don't have the money, then we should be out on the streets begging." Her eyes crinkle at the corners as she smiles again and shakes her head. She thinks I'm exaggerating.

"I mean it, Ayesha," I tell her, infusing some enthusiasm into my voice. "Maybe next year." But what good is a boundary wall when in the dead of summer afternoons young boys from the colony, impervious to the unyielding heat, will carry bricks off one by one to use as wickets when they play cricket on the main roads of the colony? Gradually, imperceptibly, like other solitary walls housing empty lots, ours too will become irregular, misshapen, and will slowly diminish in size. Then we will be expected to repair and rebuild.

I bend over and kiss the child's cheek that smells of sweat, milk, and the mustard oil Ayesha uses in her hair. "But what about you?" I ask my cousin. "When are you going to stop having children?" Ayesha is pregnant, although, being stocky, she doesn't show as yet.

Again the sheepish smile. "Ai hai, what can I do? It's God's will." Ayesha's hair is thickly patched with gray, a sight completely at odds with her chubby, unlined face. She raises long, black brows, tilts her head to one side and sighs. Her mouth, which is tiny, stretches in a grin. Her face doesn't seem to belong to the body below it, nor does the smile, waiflike and naive, appear to have anything to do with bearing unwanted children.

"But you can help me, Zenab." Her tone changes. "Only you can help me," she says tremulously.

"How?" I ask in amazement. "Do you need pills?"

She shakes her head vigorously. "No, no, that's not what I meant. I mean if only my husband could go to Amreeka . . ." She breaks off helplessly.

"What?" I start laughing, then realize she's on the verge of tears.

"Well," she continues with a sniffle, "if he isn't here there won't be any more children and perhaps he'll also find better work in Amreeka."

"But what about birth control?"

"Rafique says we shouldn't interfere with God's will, you know what he's like." The child in Ayesha's alms has fallen asleep. She rocks back and forth as she talks in a whisper. "How are we going to raise four children, provide the girls' dowries, pay for their education?"

"Someone has to drill some sense into his head, Ayesha, Amreeka isn't the answer to anyone's problems." And I embark on a lecture about keeping husbands in line.

"Zenab, I've tried, " Ayesha says earnestly, "I've tried so hard, but he has such stubborn ideas about everything."

Ammi walks into the kitchen with my three boys in tow.

"Come on everybody, it's time for breakfast . . . children, go to the dining room . . . Ramzan, here take these vegetables and put some water on for tea and hand me the frying pan . . . Zenab, finish your tea . . . it's cold, why do you let it get cold? Such nice bhindi today, just look at it . . . Zenab get your children up here at once . . . everyone

65

should have breakfast at the same time. The cleaning will start soon. Zenab, go in with your sons, see that they eat properly."

I marvel at the energy my mother exhibits. Mine is drained already, although it's only nine in the morning and the only activity I've engaged in since waking up has been the trip to the bathroom and later the walk to the kitchen.

The three boys, still groggy and upset they have been awakened so early, stagger toward the dining room like zombies, their hair awry, their faces puffed up and sullen. I follow them, wondering again if there will be any rain today. July is coming to a close and monsoons should bring the city a reprieve soon, unless something has really changed, unless something as predictable as the monsoon downpour is no longer the same. I peer hesitatingly at the sky through the dining room window, a little afraid, a little hopeful, like a young woman sneaking a look at her prospective bridegroom. The sky, stretched taut and unrelenting, is white and clear, a disappointment. The glare rankles in my eyes like sand and I pull back. I yearn for rain, I have the monsoon blues.

"Mom can we fly kites today?" Haider, bleary eyed, asks.

"Yes Mom, can we please?" Asghar and Kasim reiterate energetically with one voice. In some things at least they're united.

"But it's too hot on the roof at this time of day." I'm troubled that I have to say no.

"Please Mom, Ammi, we can't do anything else, there's nothing else to do. We can't go out because it's too hot, we can't play in the lawn because it's too hot, why did we come?" Asghar, twelve now and always questioning, grumbles, noisily bangs a spoon on the checkered plastic tablecloth and scowls.

"You know why. Anyway, eat your breakfast and then we'll see."

"We'll see, we'll see, that means no." Kasim sticks out his lower lip and his whole face falls like a collapsed soufflé and in the very next moment his eyes fill with tears. His older brothers exchange cynical glances.

"Don't start, Kasim, eat your paratha, Nanima took so much trouble to make these for you, and when it's cooler, you can go up with Ramzan. He'll get some kites and help you fly them."

Ramzan, standing nearby with a plate heaped with perfectly round, sticky-brown parathas, nods.

"Could we walk to our lot then?" Kasim asks, a spoon raised in the air.

"Yes, later." Where are the monsoons? I ask myself angrily as if I had a secret rendezvous with them, as if they had made a promise and retracted. I'll have to let the boys go. Around five in the evening they finally make the trek to the roof in the company of Ramzan and three large, multicolored tissue-paper kites that look so fragile it's a wonder they can go up at all without ripping into shreds. Ramzan gingerly holds them aloft, and like the Pied Piper, he leads the boys to the roof.

Ammi and I stand at the foot of the dark, winding cement staircase and anxiously watch the children disappear, hearing only snatches of their excited chatter as they talk to Ramzan in broken Urdu.

"Ammi, let's go and sit down for a while." I tug at my mother's sleeve.

She follows me into the family room, her thin, sparse brows curled with concern.

"They're so wild, your boys," she says.

The sofa on which I sit has been upholstered for the third time in fifteen years, in blue woven tapestry now. The long, heavy drapes on the french windows, also new, have been drawn to let in some air. But the air is as distressing as everything else around us—the seat of the sofa which seems to emit heat, the abrasive touch of my cotton shirt against my skin, the hair on the nape of my neck which feels like fur, the steaming third cup of tea in my hand.

Perspiration gathers on my face like a thin film of oil. My thoughts wander to the unwalled parcel of land with which my connection is becoming more and more tenuous, to the yellowed lifelessness in my mother's eyes.

"Did you see the house across the street from us?" she asks, her gaze pinned to some point above my person.

67

"Yes, who are the owners, do you know them?"

Ammi shifts in her seat. In spite of a meager breeze from the ceiling fan that whirs so fast the blades are just arcs of light, tiny beads of sweat have gathered on her forehead.

"A retired railway officer and his wife. Sometimes she comes over to see me."

"And the children?"

"They're not here. Two sons are in America, and the daughter, she's married and lives in Karachi. Only last month the mother was sick and the daughter flew in from Karachi in a few hours."

A heavy silence, as rough as a cloak of coarse wool, falls over us.

Ammi rubs an imaginary stain on the arm of the sofa. "You should build your boundary wall now, Zenab," she says quietly.

It's my turn to seek an imaginary spot on the arm of the sofa. "Hmm, yes," I murmur.

"The council is threatening to reclaim the land if people don't build. The idea was to populate a new colony, not have people buy lots and disappear. Your investment will go down the drain." Her hands, small-fingered with blue veins on the back that remind me of old scars, rise and fall as she speaks.

"I know, but we can't rush into this," I say, my voice rising just a notch. "Suppose we change our mind and decide not to build at all."

Ammi's eyes move restlessly and I notice for the first time that her left eyelid is drooping, giving the face a melancholy look.

"But what is this laziness, Zenab? You should go and see the plot at least, it's yours isn't it? Why did you buy it?" She emits a tight, shallow cough. She's angry.

"It was a mistake, we shouldn't have been so impetuous. But we would be making another mistake if we rush into this construction."

She coughs again, then wipes her brow with a corner of her white chiffon dupatta and points to the window. "Look, do you see those clouds in that corner? That means we'll have rain soon."

All I can see is a minute cluster of fluff, which, in the enormity of the whitewashed, pale sky is like a forgotten speck of dirt on a mirror.

"That's nothing!" I exclaim.

"Don't be silly," Ammi scolds, "you're too impatient."

Around seven Phupi Alima and Uncle Shah come to visit. The sun hasn't relinquished its place on the horizon, but is spent, dulling the sharpness of the heat somewhat. We sit in the family room where the air from the ceiling fan isn't as humid now as it was in the afternoon.

Phupi Alima is my father's youngest sister. When I was five, she taught me the names of colors in English from *The Radiant Reader Book One* in which two children, Jack and Jane, forever hopped and skipped on cobbled walks winding through English gardens adorned with vividly yellow daffodils, white-speckled daisies, clusters of violet hyacinths, purple and yellow round-petalled pansies, bold red poppies, and multicolored primroses. Phupi Alima was eighteen that year and in love with a cousin who was studying to be an engineer, and I was her first student.

Each year during my visits to her house, we spend long afternoons in the guest room, chatting tirelessly over cups of tea and meat-filled samosas, forgetting she's nearing fifty and I'm thirty-something. Today I notice that the creases on her brow have thickened, and around the corners of her mouth are cobweb-thin lines I don't remember seeing before. I've been waiting for her.

"Zenab, you haven't changed," she says as we hug.

I point to the gray strands in my hair no one can see because I've dyed them and shake my head. "But I have," I protest, laughing. Sometimes I think I wait for her with childlike eagerness so she can see me and say, "Zenab, you haven't changed."

"Well, if you have, I can't see it." She holds my hand and looks at me closely, then pats my cheek. "No, you're the same."

"Nobody is the same any more Phupi ji, and nothing is the same. Take Lahore. Was it ever so dusty and so dry?"

"Well, this is progress, my dear. The government is digging up roads to lay down fiber-optic wires so people can have telephones without the long waits." She has a derisory smile on her face.

"Well, why not, we're not to be left behind in the race for progress, are we?" Uncle Shah remarks with a snicker.

"I agree," I say. "So, what will it be? Tea? Squash?" I know it will be tea for Phupi Alima and mango squash for Uncle Shah. I run out to tell Ramzan, who's in the kitchen again preparing bhindi for dinner. A bitter-sweet, mellow vegetable smell pervades the kitchen. Amma, I discover, is taking a bath. The children are on the front lawn, playing cricket, Ramzan informs me, and only one kite went up. "We'll try again tomorrow," he adds with a smile of reassurance, knife poised in one hand, a small green okra pod held securely in the other.

On my return to the family room I find Phupi Alima and Uncle Shah contemplative. The heat is enervating so that even talking is an effort and slipping into uneasy silences is easy.

"And how is Navid? He has written he will be moving to another house in a month. Have you seen his new house?" Uncle Shah idly fingers the corners of his crisp, white malmal kurta and raises eyebrows in query.

Navid is Phupi Alima's oldest son. There aren't that many of us left here. She is bitter. She hasn't let me forget I was among the first to go to America and the first to cancel plans to return. "You and your husband have set a bad example for all the young people in the family," she said accusingly once, "telling them it's all right to abandon their parents to lives of loneliness in their big empty houses." Her voice frightened me; I felt I was a little girl again, stuttering and stammering with answers in response to her questions, confusing blue with purple, red with orange.

"Navid is fine, and so is Saima, they're so excited about the new house. And Phupi ji, they'll finally have an extra room so now you have absolutely no excuse not to come to the States." Phupi Alima has been stubbornly avoiding the trip for three years.

Ramzan brings in tea, squash in a jug, and a plate of white burfi speckled with pistachio bits. Phupi Alima waits for me to pour tea in her cup. "We'll see," she says with a sigh. "So, when are you building your wall?" The question comes as a surprise. I had forgotten about the wall, about the lot.

"Perhaps next year," I say hesitatingly, extending the cup toward her.

"What? Next year?" She jumps at me sharply. "If you don't start building the land will be taken away from you, child." Like the refrain of a song, the words follow me. She gives me a wounded look, as if I had violated a promise yet again. Setting the cup down on the table before her, she wipes her face with a corner of her green dupatta and shakes her head.

I know she's upset. Like Ammi and Ayesha, she'd like me to build quickly. Why wait, they're all saying. "Yes, I've been told about that." I stir the ice cubes in the tall glass of mango squash before handing it to Uncle Shah.

She becomes agitated and fidgets in her seat. "No, no, my child, you can't wait, there's no more time. Do you know, we've already constructed ours."

"But you're not putting a house on the lot, are you?"

"No, the land is for Navid, he can do what he wants with it when he comes back. At least no one will take it away." She's drinking her tea slowly, a chunk of burfi in one hand, the cup in the other.

"But is he coming back to live here?" The question falls from my mouth as if it were a morsel that had to be spat out. I hadn't meant for it to sound the way it did, cruel. Helplessly I look at Uncle Shah who has finished his mango drink and is now busily wiping his face with a sparkling white handkerchief.

The smile freezes on Phupi Alima's face. "If he doesn't, then his mother is dead for him." Tears gather in her eyes, her lips quiver. "You can tell him that." She wipes her eyes with her dupatta.

"Phupi ji, now don't cry, please." My eyes smart with unshed tears. We can easily have a weeping session, and Ammi will join us, gladly.

"So Zenab, when are you coming to have dinner with us?" Uncle Shah asks me, ignoring my remark, ignoring Phupi Alima's tears.

"Friday. Is that all right Phupi ji?" I turn with relief to Phupi Alima who is biting into the burfi intently.

She smiles. "Of course it's okay, any day is all right my dear. I'll make kulfi, you like kulfi, I know."

The last of the sun has dipped into the horizon when Phupi Alima and Uncle Shah leave. The veranda is darkly gray. As the three of us come out on the porch, I notice there are still no signs of clouds in the sky. Only inky darkness sprayed with the glitter of stars. And a sliver of a bright, yellow moon.

Moths flutter and dash agitatedly against the naked light bulb attached to a long wire dangling from the ceiling in the porch. The clattering of frogs, grasshoppers, and other night creatures has gained momentum. The air, still and burdened with lingering evening heat, is thick with the incense of raat ki rani, July roses and cambeli from Ammi's summer garden.

"Well, Zenab my dear, we'll see you then." Uncle Shah slips behind the wheel of his immaculately kept white Toyota. I notice that the flesh on his lean cheeks hangs in loose folds, and his deep-set eyes have sunk further back into their sockets. I remember his taut smile, his aloofness and his severe manner when we were children and Phupi Alima had just been married. But that was many years ago, and he was a civil servant then.

"Khuda hafiz." I clutch my aunt's hand before she gets into the car. Her hand is warm, the skin roughened, corrugated to the touch. In the dark her eyes shine the way they did when she was eighteen, when she was my first teacher.

"Khuda hafiz." I keep waving although I know they can no longer see me.

Ayesha has come out on the porch, her daughter straddled on her hip.

"Let's walk to your plot, Zenab," she says.

"Walk all the way with her in your arms?" I ask, wondering how, with a ten-month-old baby in her arms and another inside her, she can contemplate a long walk at this time of night.

The children have gone indoors to watch TV and gulp down bottles of Coca-Cola Ammi has kept chilled for them in her refrigerator.

"I work around the house all day long with her straddled on my hip," Ayesha remarks with a laugh. "Let's go to your plot."

"It's still too hot," I mumble. The words are like blinking an eyelash or breathing, always with you, always meaningful, necessary. If only it would rain.

"We'll go tomorrow," I hedge, "maybe we'll have rain tomorrow."

"All right, come and sit here for a while. Inside, the house is like an oven." Ayesha points to a rope cot in the far corner of the porch.

Darkness falls here in its truest sense, like an unwieldy blanket, cumbersome with the weight of stillness, its oppressive touch tangible upon one's skin, upon the grass which is already sere from the July sun, upon the gray cement walls of my parents' new home, upon Ammi's rose bushes which will flower wildly in March when I'll be in Connecticut wondering if there's going to be more snow. Upon Ayesha and her baby.

In the encroaching darkness I can't see the gray in Ayesha's hair, nor the look in her eyes, and the child's honey-brown face is also turned away from me. I hear Ammi calling Ramzan, the voice I hear thinned and weakened by distance. Soon Abba will be home from his clinic. Each time the city is deluged during the monsoons, Abba's clinic is flooded with water overflowing from the low-lying streets, and he has to stay home. That's when he takes my children out for rides in the car, a trip to the zoo, the Fortress, Shalimar Gardens, the Lahore Museum, and Kasim gets a new toy. The memory is deeply etched in my mind, yet I'm impatient.

Closing my eyes, I rest my back against Ayesha's as she croons absently to her daughter, rocking to the languid rhythm of her lullaby. I want to rise from the charpai and walk to the gate, and out, towards the lot which will have soaked the day's fever and will now be drenched with torrid vapors. There won't be much to see, I know, but I must go . . . I must go . . .

Getting up, saying nothing to Ayesha who won't move for fear of waking her sleeping child, I lumber toward the wrought-iron gate only to find it shut, padlocked. But, within seconds, the lock hangs open of its own accord, like a mouth gaping in surprise. I free the latch from it's hook, and force it to yield, the bolt squeaking as if each movement were a jab in the heart. Over a clump of mulberry bushes in Ammi's garden, I see the moon suspended in the sky like a pale gold half-disk cleverly stitched to an indigo-blue dupatta.

The gate is ajar. I leave the porch to come out on the unlighted road that will take me to my lot in ten minutes. Feeling as if I've travelled this route a hundred times, I quickly turn left and start walking. On my face the darkness is suddenly cool, wet with moisture I hadn't known about. In the absence of streetlights, a rarity in the new colony, the moon's half disk offers some illumination. But soon, beneath my feet, the dirt road, gnarled with uneven gravel, stones and sodden brick ends, becomes darker than the sky overhead. The moon fails to light my path.

At a pile of new bricks and earth, which is only a misshapen mound in the darkness, I make another turn and continue walking. The houses strung on both sides of the road and shrouded in fogged shadows are silent. I wonder about the silence and then tell myself, as if I am torn in half to become two people, that everyone is asleep at this hour.

Finally my destination appears before me, all one-tenths of an acre of it. On crossing the road I find myself at the point where the road, which will one day qualify as a boulevard, merges carelessly with the western boundary of the lot. I notice a tree. Why didn't someone tell me a tree had been planted here? I come closer. It's a large tree, a peepal perhaps, or maybe an overgrown, dense poplar. With little notice the moon takes off somewhere and it's dark again.

As if it had sat there all this while and I had merely failed to notice it the first time because of the darkness, is the veranda of the old house. In a corner at the farthest end of the small lot, it is directly across from me and distanced from the tree under which I stand. I see it clearly now. It seems to have been sliced out of the house in Garhi Shahu and transplanted in its entirety on my lot. And on a charpai, sharply visible in the light from a naked ceiling bulb swinging from a fly-infested wire is Dadima, my grandmother, Phupi Alima's mother. She's alive, I tell myself wonderingly.

"Come here, Zenab," she's saying, her voice ringing in my ears like the echoes of a distant bell.

"Is it *Yusuf Zuleikha* Dadima?" I run to sit beside her on the bed. A cool breeze moves across my face and ripples through my hair. Henna, golden yellow like the skin of winter tangerines, covers all of Dadima's hair; her narrow shoulders are hunched forward, a black shawl draped over them loosely. A book sits in her lap. A book with amber pages and olive-green covers edged with a gold lining. I can even see the script, the couplets jumping at me with blinding clarity.

"I'm going to read now, so be still, child." She wets her forefinger and pauses, before lifting the corner of the page.

I edge forward. "Are you going to read the part about Yusuf's brothers?" On Dadima's woolen shawl the familiar paisley forms, inverted in pairs, look like birds in embrace.

"No, I'm reading the part where Yusuf's father, the prophet Yaqub, has become blind from crying for his lost son. Remember? And he's been told the king of Egypt wants his next favorite son in exchange for grain? Remember?" Dadima's eyes, glazed over with age, peer closely at my face.

"Yes, I remember, I remember, read, read some more," I beseech like a child, tugging at a corner of her black shawl.

"All right, all right, don't talk now," she admonishes. "Here, get under the covers and listen quietly."

And Yaqub thrashed his breast
As tears flowed from his visionless eyes.
He lamented, crying like a child,
I will not give away my beloved son.

My eyes fill for Yaqub. For his loss, for his loneliness. I cover my

75

face and cry with a girl's abandon, tears trickling thickly through the gaps between my fingers like rain seeping through the slackened joints of an old window frame.

The words of the poem become tangled with each other, jumbled; Dadima's voice grows faint and soon all I can hear is a whisper. Anxiously I move closer to her and still I cannot hear. My chest constricts with a stabbing pain, then with some emotion that pushes aside my breath.

Her hand is on my arm. "Did you build your wall yet, child?" she's asking, her head lifted toward me, her old woman's voice suddenly loud in my ears.

I look closely at my grandmother's face through the film of moisture in my eyes. "No, no I didn't," I answer between sobs, wiping my cheeks with my palms, dragging my hand across my face fiercely. "But I will, I will."

Dadima lifts the book from her lap and holds it out to me. "Take this, Zenab," she instructs simply, "and turn off the light when you leave."

On my grandmother's face are lines I contemplate with surprise. Tiny, yet deep, forming a web, they remind me of the skeleton of a leaf gnawed through by a persistent gypsy moth, its veins drained of chlorophyll, white.

"Can I stay?" I lean toward her, my hand closing tightly on the edge of her shawl, my eyes heavy again with unshed tears.

Pulling the shawl from her shoulders, Dadima raises it with one hand while with the other she pats the bedsheet, her long thin fingers, knotted at the joints, so much like my own, aflutter with the movement of her hand. "Come," she says.

Unable to move, I sit on the charpai that squeaks noisily as Ayesha rocks back and forth with the child in her lap, and wonder if the monsoons will gather in the muted silence of the night. Will I suddenly wake up and hear the rain thrashing upon the walls of my room like urgent hands on a door? And, as I hurriedly leave my bed to shut the window casements and a sprinkle of rain alights on my face, will the room be filled with the heady aroma of wet, rained-on earth? And will I finally, in the aftermath of the deluge, get to see my lot? And what will I find there?

Ayesha's baby stirs in her lap. "Hmm . . . Hmm . . ." she croons, her eyes half shut.

In my ears my grandmother's recitation resounds faintly, like a faraway, failing sound. And the blind prophet's face, resembling the face of an old man from a Biblical film, perhaps that of Charlton Heston's Moses, fills my vision. I look at the sky for the clouds that don't come. I see nothing.

Paths Upon Water

Nothing had come along to prepare her for her first encounter with the sea. At breakfast that morning, her son said, "Apaji, we're going to the seaside today and Rashid and Hamida are coming with us."

She had been turning over a paratha in the frying pan, an onerous task since she had always made parathas on a flat skillet with open sides. As the familiar aroma of dough cooking in butter filled her son's apartment, she thought, anxiously, Why does he want to take me to the sea?

Khadija had never seen the sea. Since she had lived most of her life in a town that was nearly a thousand miles from the nearest shoreline, her experience of the sea was limited to what she had chanced to observe in pictures. One picture, in which greenish blue waves heaved toward an overcast sky, she remembered well. It was from a calendar Kamal brought home one year when he was in college in Lahore. The calendar had stayed on the wall facing her bed for many years and was removed only when the interior of the house was whitewashed for her daughter's wedding. In the ensuing confusion it was misplaced and never found. But the rusting, orange nail by which the calendar had hung all these years stayed in the wall; the painter, too lazy to bother with detailed preparations, had simply painted around the nail and over it. Every night, when she settled in bed, Khadija's gaze strayed faithfully to the stubborn nail, reminding her of what had once been there.

Also clear in her memory was a scene from an Urdu film she had seen with her sister and her niece Zenab during a summer visit to Lahore. For some reason she couldn't put the scene out of her mind. On a brown and gray beach, the actor Waheed Murad, now dead but then affectedly handsome and boyish with a cap of curly hair on his small head and a smile that often seemed forced, energetically pursued the actress Zeba. She skipped and hopped some distance ahead of him not as if she were a young woman with full breasts and rounded hips, but a little girl on her first trip to the ocean. It wasn't proper at all that a woman be running about playfully in a public place. Compact foam-crested waves lapped up to her, making her shalwar stick to her skinny legs, exposing the outline of her calves. Why, it was just as bad as baring her legs, for what cover could the gossamer-like fabric of the shalwar provide?

The two frolicked by an expanse of water that extended to the horizon and which, even though it was only on film, seemed to Khadija frightening in its immensity.

"I say, son, will Rashid and his wife have lunch here?" she asked, depositing the dark, glistening paratha in her son's plate. She would have to take out a packet of beef from the freezer if they were. Slowly she poured tea in Kamal's cup. He wants to show me the wonders of Amreeka, she told herself reassuringly, trying to quell her restiveness.

"No, I don't think so, we'll leave before lunch and stop somewhere along the way for a pizza or something." He broke off a large morsel of paratha and, rolling it, slowly filled his mouth with it.

"They'll have tea then." She was glad Kamal had picked up a cake, which he had oddly called a "pound" cake, at the store the night before. She would also make some kheer. Pizza or no pizza, the guests must be fed when they are here.

If she had her way Khadija would avoid making long trips altogether. It wasn't that she didn't like being outdoors. No, that was not it at all. Every morning she went down to the lawn to examine her surroundings, breathe the fresh clean air, and look at the sky which always seemed to stretch like an inverted ocean, the clouds billowing gently like quiet, faraway waves. She thought that the world outside Kamal's apartment was wondrous indeed. Each window was bordered on the outside of the building, she observed during one such outing, with narrow white shutters which reminded her of icing on a cake she once saw in a bakery window. And, on the face of the building the glossy white paint appeared impervious to the effects of the elements; not a discoloration was visible anywhere, nor a crack, and she had craned her neck all the way during her scrutiny.

The lawn itself, edged with freshly green, sculptured bushes, was evenly thick with grass that seemed more like a velvet carpet. Located in a quiet section of town where she never heard the tooting of horns or the screeching of car tires, or the "phat, phat" of motor rickshaws, the familiar cacophony of life in her town, the apartments overlooked a densely green wooded area where the trees grew so tall they seemed to be reaching for the sky. A park, Kamal said. Although tired and groggy the first evening of her arrival from Pakistan, Khadija had not failed to survey her surroundings with a knowing eye.

The next morning she looked out the bedroom window and was gladdened at the thought of her son's good fortune. The morning sky was clear and everything was so clean. Was it not as if an unseen hand had polished the sidewalks and swept the road? Where do people throw their filth, she wondered when she went to the lawn the first time. With her gaze she reached out to the shiny road, the rows and rows of neat houses across the road hedged in by neat, white wooden fences. In hasty answer to her own query she told herself not to be foolish. This was Amreeka. Here garbage was in its proper place, hidden from view and no doubt disposed of in an appropriate manner. No blackened banana peels redolent with the odor of neglect here, or rotting orange skins, or worse, excrement and refuse to pollute the neighborhood and endanger human habitation. No empty bloated plastic bags floating around like lost birds with nowhere to go. No, she didn't mind going out. But why go any further than the lawn, unless it was to visit her niece Fatima or the other relatives? Long trips were not for her and she wanted to spend most of her time in her son's apartment, cooking his meals and watching him eat.

She had sighed in contentment. Happiness made her lightheaded. Once again she thanked Allah.

"Is the sea far from here?" she asked casually, brushing imaginary crumbs from the edges of her plate. Kamal must never feel she didn't place a value on his eagerness to show off to her this place he was calling home. If he wanted to take her to the seaside, then seaside it would be. She was not about to be difficult and place stones in his path.

"No Apaji," Kamal said, "an hour and a half's drive altogether. You are all right, aren't you?" He glanced at her, the corners of his eyes drooping in concern as he put aside the newspaper he had been reading.

She impatiently waved a hand in the air. Secretly she was pleased at his solicitude. "Yes, yes, I'm all right. What's going to happen to me, hunh? Now finish your tea and I'll make you another cup." Khadija knew how much her son liked tea. Before she came he was making it himself. Such a chore if a man must make his own tea.

The subject of the sea didn't come up again until Rashid and his new bride arrived. Rashid, an old college friend of Kamal's, angular like him, affable and solicitous, was no stranger to Khadija. But this was her first meeting with his wife Hamida. Like herself, the girl was also a newcomer to this country.

"Khalaji, the sea's so pretty here," Hamida informed Khadija over tea, her young, shrill voice rising and falling excitedly, her lips, dark and fleshy with red lipstick, wide open in a little girl's grin, "and the beaches are so-o-o-o large, so different from the dirty beaches in Karachi." There's wanderlust in her eyes already, Khadija mused, trying to guess her age. Twenty-one or twenty-two. She thought of the girl in Lahore she and her daughter had been considering for Kamal.

81

Is there really a resemblance? Perhaps it is only the youthfulness.

"Well child, for me it will be all the same. I've never been to Karachi. Here, have another slice of cake, you too Rashid, and try the kheer."

For no reason she could understand, sitting next to the young woman whose excitement at the prospect of visiting the seaside was as undisguised as a child's preoccupation with a new toy, Khadija was suddenly reminded of the actress Zeba. The image of waves lapping up to her legs and swishing about her nearly bare calves rose in her mind again. Like the sudden arrival of an unexpected visitor, a strange question crossed her mind: Are Hamida's legs also skinny like Zeba's?

Drowned in the clamor for the kheer, which proved an instant success and was consumed with such rapidity that she wished she had made more, the question lost itself.

"Khalaji, you must tell Hamida how you make this," Rashid was saying, with longing in his voice, and Hamida quickly interjected with, "You've used extra milk, haven't you Khalaji?"

"Yes, yes, child, have more," Khadija said with a smile.

Tea didn't last very long. Within an hour they were on their way, all of them in Kamal's new red Toyota in which the black upholstery was slippery to the touch and carried an intrusive smell of car oil. Rashid sat in the front with his friend while Khadija and Hamida were in the back, an unfortunate arrangement, as Khadija discovered after they had driven for what seemed to her like an hour. It wasn't Hamida's ceaseless prattle that vexed her, she realized, it was her perfume. So pungent, she could feel it wafting into her nostrils, it irritated the inside of her nose, and then traveling down to her throat, rankled there like the acrid aftertaste of an overripe orange. But her discomfort was short-lived because soon she became drowsy and idled into sleep.

*

Khadija had heard stories of people who swam in the sea. She was not stupid. She knew swimming was not undertaken fully clothed. After all, as a child she had often seen young boys and men in her village swim, dressed in nothing but loincloths as they jumped into the muddy waters of the canal that irrigated their fields. But what was this?

As soon as Kamal parked his car in a large, compoundlike enclosure fenced in by tall walls of wire mesh, and when her dizziness was assuaged somewhat, Khadija glanced out of the window on her left, her attention drawn to what she thought was a naked woman. Certain that she was still a little dazed from the long drive, her vision subsequently befogged, Khadija thought nothing of what she had seen. An illusion, that's what it is. Then the naked figure moved. Disbelief gave way to the sudden, disturbing realization that the figure was indeed real, and if not altogether naked, very nearly so.

A thin strip of colored cloth shaped like a flimsy brassiere loosely held the woman's breasts, or rather a part of her breasts; below that, beneath the level of her belly button, no, even lower than that, Khadija observed in horror, was something that reminded her of the loincloths the men and youths in her village wore when they swam or worked on a construction site in the summer.

The girl was pretty. Such fine features, hair that shone like a handful of gold thread, and she was young too, not much older than Hamida, Khadija was sure. But the paleness of her skin was marred by irregular red blotches that seemed in dire need of a cooling balm. No one with such redness ought to be without a covering in the sun, Khadija offered silent rebuke.

The women opened the door of her car, which was parked alongside Kamal's, on the right, and as she bent down to retrieve something from the interior of the car, Khadija gasped, covering her mouth with her palm in disbelief. When the young female lowered her body, her breasts were not nearly all bared but stood in imminent danger of spilling out of their meager coverage. O God! Is there no shame here? Khadija's cheeks burned. Hastily she glanced away. In the very next

83

instant she sneaked a glimpse at her son from the corner of her eyes, anxiously looking for some signs of discomfort on his part; no, she noted with a mixture of surprise and relief, he and Rashid were taking things out of the trunk of the car with no visible signs of distress. As a matter of fact, they seemed not to be aware of this vision of nakedness. But was that a fleeting look of curiosity on Hamida's face, a flustered smile? There was something else too the older woman couldn't quite decipher.

Relieved that her male companions were oblivious to the unseemly view of the woman's breasts, Khadija sighed sadly. She shook her head, adjusted her white chiffon dupatta over her head, and slowly eased her person out of her son's car.

The taste of sea was upon her lips instantly. Mingled with an occasional but strong whiff of Hamida's perfume, the smell of fish quickly settled in her nose as if there to stay forever.

Countless groups of scantily clad people milled about her; men, women, and children came and went in all directions, toward her and away from her. Is all of Amreeka here? she asked herself uneasily. Troubled by a feeling of guilt because she had judged Zeba's contrived imprudence on film a little too harshly, she tightened her head-covering about her as if it were a shawl, and wondered why Kamal had chosen this place among all others to bring her to. Didn't he know his mother? But she was an old woman, the mother of a son. She wouldn't surrender to annoyance or scorn and embarrass her son. His poise and confidence were hers too, were they not? Certainly he had brought her to the sea for a purpose. She must not appear impatient or intolerant.

While Rashid and Kamal walked on ahead of them, casually and without any show of awkwardness, laughing and talking as if they were in their drawing room rather than a place crowded with people in a state of disconcerting undress, she and Hamida followed closely behind. Hamida was unusually quiet. Khadija's head swam for a moment as she averted her gaze from the sun and attempted to scrutinize the perturbing nakedness around her.

Khadija's memories of nakedness were short and limited, extending to the time she had bathed her younger brother and sister under the water pump in the courtyard of her brother's house, followed by the period in which she had bathed her own children until they were old enough to do it themselves. Of her own nakedness she carried an incomplete image; she had always bathed sitting down, on a low stool.

Once, and that too shortly before his stroke, she came upon her husband slipping out of his dhoti in their bedroom. He stood absently near the foot of his bed as if waiting for something or someone, the dhoti a crumpled heap about his bony ankles. When she entered the room he lifted his face to look at her blankly, but made no attempt to move or cover himself. Not only did she have to hand him his shalwar, she also had to assist him as he struggled to pull up first one leg and then the other and tied the drawstring with fumbling hands. A week later he suffered a stroke, in another week he was gone. It had been nearly ten years since his death. But for some reason the image of a naked, disoriented man in the middle of a room clung to her mind like permanent smudges on a well-worn copper pot.

And there was too, unforgettable, the sharp and unsullied picture of her mother's body laid out on a rectangular slab of cracked, yellowed wood for a preburial bath, her ashen brown skin laced with a thousand wrinkles, soft, like rained-on mud. Sunlight in the courtyard of her father's house filled the crevices of her mother's nakedness like tiny silver rivulets irrigating a plowed and seeded field.

But nothing could have prepared Khadija for this. Nakedness, like all things in nature, has a purpose, she said solemnly to herself as the four of them trudged toward the water.

The July sun on this day was nowhere as searing as the July sun in Lahore, but a certain oily humidity had begun to attach itself to her face and hands. With a corner of her dupatta she wiped her face, ignoring the brown streaks that formed on the clean, white surface as she brushed it across her cheeks. Poor Hamida, no doubt she too longed to divest herself of the shalwar and kameez she was wearing and don a swimming suit so she could join the rest of the women on the beach, be more like them. But can she swim?

They continued onward. After some initial plodding through hot, moist sand, Khadija grew sure-footed and was soon able to tread over the weighty sand with relative ease. No more dragging of the feet for her. She looked about her now. It wasn't long before she realized that she and Hamida were drawing stares, some vaguely curious, some unguardedly inquisitive.

Where the bodies ended, she saw, the ocean began, stretching to the horizon in the distance. The picture she had carried in her head of the boyish actor Waheed Murad running after a petulantly girlish Zeba on a sandy Karachi beach quickly diminished and faded away. The immensity of the sea on film was reduced to a mere splash of color, its place usurped by a vastness she could scarce hold within the frame of her vision. In her head a window opened, she breathed in the wonder of the sea as it touched the hem of the heavens. Despite the heat, Khadija shivered involuntarily. Allah's touch is on man's world.

Again and again, as she had made preparations for her journey, she had been told Amreeka was so large many Pakistans could fit into it. The very idea of Pakistan fitting into anything else was cause for bewilderment, it was surely ludicrous, and the analogy left her befuddled and awed. But had she expected this?

The bodies sprawled before her on the sand and exposed to the midday sun's unyielding rays seemed unmindful of what the ocean might have to say about Allah's touch upon man's world. Having assumed supine positions, flat either on their backs or their bellies, the people on the beach reminded Khadija of whole red chili spread out on an old worn blanket and left out in the sun to dry and crackle. As sweat began to form in tiny droplets across her forehead and gathered around her mouth in minuscule puddles, the unhappy thought presented itself to her that she was among people who had lost their sanity. "People in Amreeka are very strange, Khadija, they say they are not like you and me." The words of her next-door neighbor echoed in her ears. How fortunate Kamal could not read her thoughts.

Your first effort in the summer is to put as much distance as possible between the sun and yourself. Every effort is made to stay indoors; curtains are drawn and bamboo screens unfurled against the fire the sun exuded. In the stray silence of a torrid June or July afternoon, even stray dogs seek shade under a tree or behind a bush, curling up into fitful slumber as the sun beats its fervid path across the sky. Khadija couldn't understand why these men and women on this beach wished to scorch their bodies. And why, if they were here, by the shore of an ocean which seemed to reach God, they did not at least gaze wide-eyed at the wonder that lay at their feet. Why did they choose instead to shut their eyes and merely wallow in the heat? Their skins had rebelled, the red-and-pink blotches spoke for themselves. Perhaps this is a ritual they must follow, perhaps they yearn to be brown as we yearn to be white.

She felt an ache putter insidiously behind her eyelids. The sun always gave her a headache, even in winter when sunshine had the facility to evoke pleasurable sensations of much-needed warmth. The heat from the sand under the dhurrie, on which she and Hamida had installed themselves, seeped through the coarse fabric after a while and cloaked her thighs. As people in varying shades of pink, white, and red skin ran or walked past them, particles of sand flew in the air and landed on her clothes, her hands, her face. Soon she felt sand in her mouth, scraping between her teeth like the remains of chewed betel nut, lying heavy on her tongue.

She decided to ignore the sand in her mouth and the hot-water effect of the sand beneath her legs and shifted her attention first toward a woman on her left, and then to the man on her right whose stomach fell broadly in loose folds like dough left out overnight. Recumbent and inert, his face covered by a straw hat, he appeared lifeless. Puzzled by the glitter on his nakedness and that of the woman on the other side, Khadija peered closely, intently; she had to observe keenly if she were to learn anything. The truth jumped at her like a sudden flash of light in a dark room. Both had smeared their bodies with some kind of oil! All at once she remembered the oversized cucumbers she had encountered in the vegetable section during her first visit to Stop and Shop; shiny and slippery, one fell from her hands as she tried to hold it within her palm. "They are greased!" she had exclaimed in disbelief to Kamal, who merely smiled indulgently..

It's really very simple. These people want to be fried in the sun. Helpless at the hands of her ignorance, Khadija sighed. But why? Not wishing to appear unenlightened, she kept her mouth shut. Even if she had addressed the query to Hamida, she was sure she would not have received a satisfactory answer. The girl was a newcomer like herself. Also, she was too young to know the answers to questions that warranted profound thought preceded by profound scrutiny. And she didn't look too comfortable either. Perhaps the heat was getting to her as well.

However, Kamal and Rashid, both in swimming shorts, appeared completely at ease as they raced to the water and back, occasionally wading in a wave that firmly slapped the beach before it ebbed out to sea again. Sometimes the boys disappeared altogether for one or two seconds under the crest of a wave rising high, and Khadija couldn't be sure anymore where they were.

She and Hamida must be the only women on the beach fully clothed, Khadija reflected, such a ludicrous sight if one were being viewed from the vantage point of the people stretched out on the sand. And while she grappled with this unnerving thought, she saw, from the corner of her eye, appearing from her right, the other woman.

Attired in a blue sari with white and red striped borders, and accompanied by a short, dark man (who had to be her son for he undoubtedly had the firm set of her jaw and her small nose), and an equally short dark woman, both of them clad in scant swimming suits. The girl's was as brief as that of the woman in the parking lot, Khadija noted with some degree of alarm. The older woman, perhaps even a year or so younger than herself, wore gold bangles on her thin wrists. Clutching the front folds of her sari, as if afraid a sudden wind from the ocean might pull them out and unfurle the sari, leaving her exposed, she trode upon the sand with a fiercely precarious step. With her gaze directed ahead, she shielded her eyes from the sharpness of sunlight with a small palm set stiffly next to the small red bindi on her forehead.

This is how I must look to the others. Suddenly Khadija felt sadness grasping at her chest, stifling her as though it were a weight that had fallen on her. The woman in the sari was making herself comfortable on a large, multicolored towel thrown hurriedly on the sand for her by her son. The young couple dashed off in the direction of the water. But why are they in such haste?

Her knees drawn, one arms tensely wrapped around them, the woman appeared to be watching only her son and daughter-in-law as they sprinted into the water. But can I be really sure? Her hand against her forehead conceals her eyes from me. As she continued to observe the woman's slight figure around which the blue cotton sari seemed to have been carelessly draped, she wondered what part of India she might be from. Could they talk to each other?

Khadija's attention returned to Hamida, who had not opened her mouth all this time. Like a sudden breakthrough during muddled thought, it occurred to her that there was a possibility Hamida would be swimming if it weren't for her. In deference to her older companion she was probably foregoing the chance to wear a bathing suit that would bare her body. Will Kamal's wife also wear a scant bathing costume and bare her body in the presence of strange men? The question rankled like a bitter aftertaste and she tried to shrug it aside. But it wouldn't go away. Stubbornly it returned, not alone this time but accompanied by the picture of a young woman who vaguely resembled the actress Zeba and who was clothed, partially, in a bathing suit much like the ones Khadija saw about her. Running behind her was a man, not Waheed Murad, alas, but her son, her dear boy Kamal. Was she dreaming? Had the sun addled her brain? Such foolishness. Khadija noted that Hamida was staring ahead, like the woman on the towel, her eyes squinted from the glare. Frozen on her bright red lips was a half smile.

Once again Khadija sought her son's figure among the throng near the water's edge. At first the dazzle of the sun blinded her and she failed to see him. She strained her eyes, shielding them with a hand on her forehead. Finally she spotted him. He and Rashid were talking to some people. The young man from India and his wife. The son and daughter-in-law of the woman in the sari. Were they acquaintances then, perhaps, friends? The four of them laughed like old friends, the girl standing so close to Kamal he must surely be unable to ignore her half-naked breasts.

They began to walk toward the spot where she and Hamida sat. Asad was going to introduce his friends to his mother. How was she to conceal her uneasiness at the woman's mode of dress?

"Apaji, this is Ajay and this is his wife Sita. Ajay works at Ethan Allen with me. Sita says she'd like you to come to their house for dinner next Sunday."

Both Ajay and Sita lifted their hands and said "Namaste," and Khadija nodded and smiled. What does one say in answer to "Namaste?"

Hamida was also introduced. Sita made a joke about the shy bride, Hamida showed her pretty teeth in a smile and played with the edges of her shirt, and then Sita said, "Auntie, you must come."

Khadija couldn't understand why Asad appeared so comfortable in the presence of a woman who was nearly all naked. Even her loincloth was flimsy. Granted it wasn't as bad as some of those others where the back was just a string that disappeared between the buttocks, but it was flimsy nonetheless.

"Yes, it's very nice of you to invite me, but it's up to Kamal, he's usually so busy, but if he's free . . ."

"Of course I'm free next Sunday, we'd love to come, Sita."

Sita said, "Good! I'll introduce you and Auntie to my mother-in-law after a swim? Coming?" She placed a hand on Kamal's arm and Khadija glanced away, just in time to catch Hamida's look of surprise. Well, one's own son can become a stranger too, even a good son like Kamal.

"Sure. Yar Ajay, are you planning to go to the Lata show in New York?"

"Yes we are. Do you have tickets?"

Ajay wasn't a bad-looking boy. But he didn't measure up to Kamal. No, Kamal's nose was straight and to the point, his forehead wide and his eyes well illuminated. But he had changed somehow. Khadija felt distanced from him. But a son is always a son. She smiled and nodded as Ajay and Sita murmured namastes and returned to the water with Kamal and Rashid.

"Khalaji, why don't we wet our feet before we go home?" Hamida's voice startled her.

"Wet our feet? Go in the water?"

"Yes Khalaji, just dip our feet, you know just get close enough to the edge? Come on, you're not afraid of a little water, are you?" Hamida's tone became playful.

"No child." No, she wasn't afraid. Her mind was playing tricks on her, filling her head with thoughts that had no place there. "Yes, why not?" she said, emboldened.

When she attempted to stand she found her joints had stiffened. "Here, girl, give me your hand," she said, extending an arm toward Hamida. Why not, especially since they had come so far and she had suffered the heat for what seemed like a very long time.

Hamida rolled up her shalwar to the level of her knees. How pretty her legs are, the skin hairless and shiny, like a baby's, and not skinny at all, Khadija mused in amazement, and how quick she is to show them!

She must do the same, she realized, if they were to go close to the water. Or Hamida might think she was afraid and surely they would look foolish too. Slowly the older woman pulled up one leg of her shalwar tentatively and tucked it at the waist with one swift movement of her hand, the way she always did when she was washing her courtyard in the house in Lahore. But this was Amreeka. She looked about her bashfully. Hamida burst out laughing.

"The other one too, Khalaji!"

Who would want to ogle at her aged and scrawny legs? And her husband was not around to glare at her in remonstration for being giddy. The other leg of the shalwar was also lifted and deftly tucked in. How funny her legs looked, the hair on them all gray and curly, the calves limp.

Kamal and Rashid laughed and waved when they saw the women approach. They are not surprised, thank God. Khadija waved back.

The front of her shalwar held cautiously between her hands, as if she really could save it from getting wet, she strode toward the water, Hamida only a few steps behind her. She smiled at the woman in the blue sari as she went past her. The woman gave her a startled look. Then, dropping the hand with which she had been shielding her eyes, she let her other arm fall away from her knees, and following Khadija with her gaze, she returned her smile.

"Wait, girl," Khadija called to Hamida who was ahead of her now. Her dupatta slipped from her head and fell in a huddle over her shoulders, her breath came fast from the exertion of her step.

"Wait," she said in a loud voice.

Chagrin

It's a Sunday in March. Not of much account because Sunday is
Sunday, the end of the weekend, the day before we all jump into work
like clocked robots, rushing toward, well, the next weekend. And
March is drab, a month when winter fights in insidious ways to show
she's mistress. It's nothing like the March in Lahore I have almost
forgotten.

Before going to bed we listened faithfully to the weather forecast
so what I see from the bedroom window this morning doesn't surprise. The sky, the tall, bare-branched, stringy trees, and our win-
ter-beaten front lawn, all seem to be wearing muted shades of the
same color: a muddied, albescant lavender. We'll wait for the sun all
day long.

"Damn!" Ali mutters, as if he didn't know and has been caught
off-guard. It's his turn at the window.

"I hope it doesn't snow," I mumble reflexively, although I know
that it might, tomorrow if not today. We should have settled in Texas
instead of Connecticut. Hot, predictable, flat, so much like the plains
of Punjab. Perhaps we can retire there.

"Islamic class today," I remind Ali as he climbs back into bed.
"One-thirty?"

93

"Yes," I say, wondering why he never remembers.

An empty plastic cover falls to the wooden floor with a sharp clang as I rummage through a scattered pile of tapes on our nightstand. Ignoring it, I select a tape and slip it into the stereo.

Zinda hun istarah ke gham-e-zindagi nahin
Jalta hua diya hun magar roshni nahin

I live with no thought to life's sorrows
I am a candle that is lit but sheds no light.

Back in bed, I draw the covers over my shoulders as the mellow tones of Mukesh's voice dart from the stereo speakers, filling the bedroom, drowning out the noise of cartoons downstairs which had woven itself into the early morning silence of our house. The children are awake.

We can't see what's outside our windows anymore; gray, brown, lavender, it can be anything and we won't know. Together, our bodies close, we listen quietly, intently, to the song. I shut my eyes and the lyrics lilt in my head, moving faster than they do on the tape, the two sounds like voices in a fugue, my head nestled in the warmth between my husband's shoulder blades, I wait greedily for the next song, then the next, and the next.

10:30 AM

"Islamic class today." The reminder is intended for the three boys who huddle together on the carpet in front of the television while Fred Flintstone and his prehistoric family with their anachronistic lifestyle yabadabadoo their way into their lethargic little heads. I hear a grunt, a "hmn". Motionless, the children sit with their mouths half-open, their eyes still glazed over from sleep, the lids heavy.

"Did you hear me?" I ask, loudly this time, forcing anger into my tone.

"Yes," Haider moans.

From the floor I retrieve a copy of *Time*, lying open, face down, embracing the carpet like a bat. On my way upstairs to the kitchen, I also pick up a stray cushion which, far from its destination on the sofa, betrays the energy generated in this room last night as the three boys wrestled, scuffled and threw things at each other.

Tea.

Ali is in the bathroom. I hear water swishing through the overhead pipes. He won't be down for another half hour. Tea, I think and "O for a draught of vintage that hath been/ Cool'd a long age in the deep-delved earth," ambles into my head. I try to dismiss Keats, but he follows me with "My heart aches and a drowsy numbness pains my sense," and in the next moment, as if I had summoned her with those words, she's in my vision. Mrs Kabir, the matronly Mrs Kabir who taught us English literature in school and who goaded us into learning by heart poems of which we were sure we would have no need later in life.

The tea kettle screeches violently.

1:30 PM

The three cars in the parking lot at Brookfield Library stand apart from each other, like the estranged members of a warring family, turning the other way, sullen.

"Well, looks like three families today," Haider mutters. Why bother when no one else does, he's telling himself. He had wanted to stay home and finish reading The *Once and Future King* for a test to-morrow. No excuses will do, I had said, bring the book along and read in the car.

"We're here, that makes four," I say firmly. But he's right. Four families for Islamic class is distressing. Sometimes we have seven or eight families which translates into ten or fifteen children. But that is rare. People have plans on weekends, no one can force anyone to come, and of course, the weather has been like a monster in a fairy story, standing in your way, demanding a heavy price for letting you pass.

The recreation room at Brookfield Library is large and bare of any furnishings that might lend it character. Two oversized prints, one with large-petalled yellow flowers that could be chrysanthemums or gardenias, another with a barn surrounded by a profusion of orange, red and brown tints and splashes meant to recreate fall, hang on the walls forlornly. It is a room which can be made to wear any disguise; for us it is the Islamic Center, for the girl scouts who meet here weekly, it's a den, for another group it's something entirely theirs. It will be anything you want it to be.

In this room, which also has an adjoining kitchen, the Center has Eid prayers followed by socializing and food, iftar gatherings during Ramzan, even birthday parties. And, despite erratic attendance, the school continues, tenaciously, stubbornly, refusing to give up.

Today there are three children attending Mr Ismail's Arabic language class. He has assigned them pages of writing, a task that seems to engross them. Slowly, laboriously, their small heads bent low over their notebooks, the children shape letters from the Arabic alphabet, struggling to maintain the right to left rhythm. The older children sit with the adults today since there aren't enough for a class. Mustafa, a Pakistani electric engineer turned handyman and builder, reads the Arabic text of sections 7 and 8 of Sura Tauba from the Koran. When he finishes, he asks Haider to read the English translation. For the first time I find out how much zakat we're supposed to give away. Two-and-a-half percent of our "merchandise," and ten percent of the "fruits of the earth."

Mustafa begins to explain the point about the fruits of the earth, and Naheed, his wife, proposes that fruits don't necessarily imply agricultural goods.

"It's everything, all the things we have and all the money we make." She looks at me when she finishes. She wants me to agree.

Fruits of the earth, fruits of labor. We might be getting into symbolism here and one man's symbolism is another man's nightmare. "I don't know," I say, "it could mean just material possessions, like real estate, jewelry, you know, things like that."

"But money is material, and what about stocks and bonds? Or could all that be merchandise?" Ali rubs down the corners of his mustache thoughtfully.

We've probably been doing it all wrong all these years. Not giving enough, or giving too much of the wrong thing. For example, old, out-of-fashion clothes dumped at the door of the Salvation Army store constitute neither merchandise nor fruits.

Mustafa looks worried. "The question is, how do we determine ten percent?" Because he was reading, he finds himself in a position to ask questions with a certain degree of authority.

Haider and Asghar, a year younger than his brother, are yawning.

"Let's read the notes," I say.

Continuing to frown, Mustafa turns to the notes at the end of the Arabic text. Silently we all wait for illumination. But none seems forthcoming. Soon it becomes clear that no one among us knows how alms are to be distributed.

"We'll have to consult the hadith," Naheed finally suggests, hitching her shoulders up and down. Her husband nods. With a sense of relief we all lean back in our seats.

"Let's go on. Asghar, will you please read the next section."

Asghar looks at me, I nod, he begins reading in a disinterested, droning voice, occasionally hindered by English transliterations of Arabic words. Suddenly he's stuck at a word. "Chagrin." ". . . the fathers whose spiritual chagrin was even worse than discomfiture in this world." Jaffer pronounces the "ch" as in "chair."

Haider snickers at his brother's mistake. Ali corrects the pronunciation, and I wonder idly if the boys know what chagrin means.

At Mr Ismail's table across the room all is quiet. Kasim, who has just turned seven, is immersed in writing. Unlike his brothers, he takes some of his work here seriously. At the moment he's copying Arabic words from a xeroxed handout. He copies well and is conscientious about what has to be done, but he doesn't know what the words mean or why he must copy them. Mr Ismail, who is Egyptian, continues, as others have done, to teach the children Arabic so they may be able to read and understand the Koran one day. He has little faith in translations because Arabic is his mother tongue. Once we tried telling him that for us a translation has done well all this time, but he was offended by our comments and implied a reluctance on our part to 'understand the true meaning of the Koran."

Asghar has finished reading. That's all we will do today. I look at the pretty blue-eyed baby in Elizabeth Smith's lap and smile at her. A look of surprise spreads on her face and then she turns her head away. I lean over and tap her cheek.

"She's so cute," I tell Elizabeth whose own eyes are darker than mine and whose hair, the little that has escaped from under her hijab, is so black I suspect she dyes it.

Elizabeth laughs. "She's a shrewd one," she says. Her voice is thick with a British accent because she and her husband have migrated from Britain recently. They are both displaced Palestinians. Her older daughter, Nadira, is on Kasim's table, writing the alphabet.

"Looks like snow." It's Naheed. Her eyes are directed to the window on the far side of the room, near the entrance.

"Oh, please!" Elizabeth and I turn to follow her gaze in alarm.

"Do you see flurries?" I ask apprehensively. I hate snow. It's so unpredictable, so hypocritical with its outward promise of beauty and its insidious power to hurt. So cold.

"No, no, it's just so dark out there." With a guilty smile Naheed pushes her glasses up her nose and I notice she has strong hands, her nails clipped short, neat.

"Well, we've had snow in late March before," Ali offers wisely. I wait for "March comes in like a lamb, goes out like a lion," but today I think he feels he doesn't have the right audience for it.

"Let's not talk about snow. I couldn't take one more day of it." I start wrapping my copy of the Koran in a cotton cloth embroidered with small round mirrors.

Haider and Asghar get up and run toward the door. Ali shuffles to his feet. Mustafa and Naheed also rise from their chairs. Mr Ismail's class is over. He walks in our direction and we all greet him with

"Salamalekum." A chorus of "How are you?" follows with jumbled, mumbled, "Fine, fine," and "Alhamdolillah."

The chairs and tables have to be put away. We must leave the room as we found it, with no traces of our visitation, our quick, reluctant learning. Amidst the metallic clitter, clatter of chairs being folded, the children, in a sudden burst of energy, begin bolting around the room, laughing, screaming. Within a few minutes, all of them, including Kasim, are embroiled in a game of tag.

4:30 PM

"Mom, what does "chagrin" mean?"

It's Asghar. We have been driving for nearly twenty minutes. "A feeling of disappointment, or sadness, like someone put you down or embarrassed you."

"Oh. I never thought I'd see a word like this in the Koran. It's weird." Asghar chuckles.

"But the Koran is full of words like this, ordinary, everyday words."

"And ordinary everyday stories too," Ali volunteers sagely.

"I know that," Asghar concedes hastily.

Ali slides a tape in the tape deck. It presses into place with a tiny click.

Mein ne samjha tha ke tu hai to darakhsaan hai hayaat
Tera gham hai to gahm-e-dehr ka jhagra kiya hai

I thought that if I were with you
Life would be glorious
That if I have your pain
The woes of the world will not torment me.

Yun na tha mein ne faqat chaha tha ke ho jae
Mujh se pehli si muhabbat mere mehbub naa maang

But that was not how it was, I had merely wished it to be thus.
Beloved, ask not for the love we once shared.

Ali turns up the volume. It is Nur Jahan singing the verses of the
poet Faiz. I hum along, "Beloved ask me not . . ." In the back, Asghar
says something, Haider breaks into a laugh, and Kasim says, with a
whine, "Tell me, tell me."

Outside our car, as we travel on Route 133 toward home, late afternoon slowly turns into dusk. The horizon is shot with crimson and
the thready limbs of tall dark leafless trees seem to be lifted up toward a darkening sky in postures of supplication. There's to be snow,
I tell myself. Slowly, the children's voices gain momentum.

All Is Not Lost

Zenab should have been shocked by the news. But she's not. Instead, she experiences a vague uneasiness, as if she has taken a wrong turn during a rushed drive to town and suddenly finds herself among unfamiliar surroundings. When she delivers the news to Phupi Khadija, who is poised at that moment to pick up the frying pan in which she has prepared the bhagar for the daal, she reacts in a way that makes Zenab feel guilty. The frying pan, small and blackened from overuse and in which the thinly sliced garlic cloves have fried and burnt to dark, crispy half-moons, leaps from Phupi Khadija's hands and lands on the kitchen floor with a muted thud.

Maryam, Cousin Shahid's daughter, is marrying an American. An *American* American. For nearly a year Phupi Khadija has coveted her for her younger son Kamal, who is twenty-five, has just received a master's degree in economics from NYU, and is looking for a high-powered job. Maryam's silky-white complexion and fine, uncomplicated nose has been in Phupi Khadija's thoughts for a long time; noses and complexions are a major preoccupation with mothers scouting for brides for their sons. On the other hand, Kamal, whose own nose tends to be somewhat on the bulbous side and whose complexion is nowhere near fair, has been hedging. Huddled together over tea, mothers and aunts wonder irately about such reticence, while sisters and cousins know the boys no longer want to be led passively into marriage. He is not ready, Kamal has told his mother, but Zenab knows that is his way of keeping his mother at bay until sparks flew for him.

"Nowadays boys know nothing about responsibility," Phupi Khadija grumbles, slapping her head with her palm in dismay the last time the subject of arranging a match for Kamal comes up in conversation.

Now Maryam is lost. And to make matters worse, an American is to have her. Phupi Khadija is inconsolable. While Zenab carefully mops up the greasy mess on the floor with kitchen towels, she hunches in her chair nearby and, a morose expression mapped on her small-boned, wrinkled face, she mutters sounds of regret under her breath.

Phupi Khadija arrived from Pakistan in May. Now, a month later, she thinks she has cause for regret.

"I knew I shouldn't have come. Why did I come? To see this happen?" She sighs, then continues, "I wonder what surprises my son has in store for me."

No doubt she has heard rumors of sparks and the like.

"Don't start worrying about Kamal, Phupi," Zenab hastens to assure her. Of course she is worried, and why not? Sitting down across from her, the crunched up oily ball of paper held tightly in her fist, Zenab brushes the perspiration from her forehead and says, "There's enough to worry about already."

"Well girl, what do you expect? When you send a young girl to work in some faraway shop with no one to keep an eye on her, what do think will come from that?"

Parveen, Maryam's mother, has been an unflaggingly diligent mother. Other cousins, whose children are younger, have watched her with reverence and awe, and a hope, voiced openly, that they too might do their job as well as she has done. She took her daughter to weekend Islamic classes, she made sure the girl fasted and said her prayers regularly, she even went so far as to tell Maryam to carry a plastic glass in her bag so that if she had to use a ladies' bathroom somewhere she'd not be put out for lack of a container for water. Such pains the woman has taken, and now this. And the weekly Islamic class, in turn, had done all it could to enforce the ideas of a woman's place, an awareness of the "small window of opportunity to find a good and right husband" as one male teacher put it, and the need for her to protect herself against the evil ways of those to whom modesty was just a joke. Parveen has entrusted Maryam to the care of wise, knowing mullahs who have devoted their lives to teaching children, serious, sad-looking men with short and long beards, intrepid counselors who have uprooted themselves from their native lands to come to America in order to keep children in the fold. And now Maryam has strayed.

Parveen is incoherent on the phone when she calls with the distressing news. At first Zenab thinks someone has died. "Parveen," she shouts into the receiver, "for God's sake, what's happened?"

"Maryam wants to marry an American boy," Parveen sobs hysterically, her voice changing into a prolonged groan. A little later, between sobs and sniffles and complaints about the hard blow fate had dealt them, she says Shahid hadn't left the house in three days. "He's threatening to kill the boy," she whimpers.

Her voice hoarse from crying, she tells Zenab that Maryam has been reprimanded severely by Shahid, but the girl refuses to be intimidated by her father's rage. "She's threatening to run away from home if we don't give our consent."

Zenab is surprised at Maryam's boldness. She had been such a subdued, docile teenager. And she always pleased Parveen's friends with the well-ordered way in which she served them tea, samosas, and gulab jamuns. "You've trained her so well," everyone told Parveen.

"We're feeling helpless," Parveen says brokenly, not listening to a word Zenab has said about being calm in a crisis.

In her senior year at school Maryam took up a job as cashier at

Shapiro's supermarket. Now she is a freshman at Rutgers University and she wants to marry Jerry Noggles, a young man who has risen from the position of stock boy to manager at Shapiro's. Phupi Khadija makes Zenab tell her the entire story twice, chaffing her plump hands and slapping her deeply lined forehead alternately as she listens. Finally, she says, "Parents are nothing, they have no control any more, and poor Shahid, he's not going to be able to show his face in the community again." She begins mumbling to herself. The channa daal, her specialty, is forgotten as is the bhagar, which she has been preparing so painstakingly. Zenab realizes she should have waited until after dinner to tell her, but that was when Ali would be home, and husbands have such little patience with gossip.

Zenab starts peeling more garlic.

"Shahid will have to agree to the wedding, that's better than an elopement, Phupi." The garlic cloves, soft and fleshy under Zenab's fingers, are white and smooth like peeled almonds.

"An elopement. Yes, that's all we need to have our noses cut." Phupi Khadija mutters unhappily under her breath.

"You wait and see," Zenab says, slicing the crescent-shaped clove evenly, "we'll be attending a wedding soon. You should start learning some English Phupi, you're the only elder here and you'll have to welcome Maryam's American in-laws at the door on the day of the wedding." The smell of garlic draws water in her mouth.

"Don't joke with me, girl," Phupi Khadija says grimly, "I'm not attending any such wedding and that Amreekan thoon thaan isn't for me. Just think what torment this will be for Shahid's father's soul."

Ah yes, Zenab thinks. Old stories, heard in childhood, come up like smoke through a vent, intrusive, difficult to ignore. Shahid's father, Uncle Kazim Ali, Fatima's father, and Phupi Khadija are all first cousins. As teenagers Phupi Khadija and Uncle Kazim Ali had made promises to each other in secret, were engaged, and then along came a family crisis rooted in someone else's bad marriage and the two were forced to go their separate ways. Phupi Khadija vowed never to marry and had to be coerced. What torment, indeed, and such helplessness.

Phupi Khadija twirls her bangles around her wrist and plucks agitatedly at her dupatta. "I'll just have to go to Shahid and Parveen right away, Shahid will need me. If these fools had stayed in their own country," she continues despondently, "none of this would have happened. Why did they leave Pakistan and come to settle in a country where your daughters are not safe from Amreekan boys?"

Zenab turns to increase the speed of the fan on the counter. June in Connecticut this year is no less oppressive than June in Lahore and there hasn't been much rain. Whatever little has fallen this month has come like some prayer being answered in installments, at an agonizingly slow pace. And, to the surprise of all Lahore visitors this year, the Connecticut sun can be as merciless as the Lahore sun. The heat from the stove is not helping matters any, either.

The bhagar is ready. Zenab turns off the stove. Dark, thin tendrils of smoke arise from the pan and a heavy smell of garlic and burnt cumin seeds fill the kitchen. Picking up the frying pan, she slowly pours the oil and garlic mixture over the daal which has been sitting patiently in the pot all this time. The bhagar bubbles furiously and foams, forming a brown and honey-gold center before subsiding. In the background is a low hum that is Phupi Khadija's lugubrious "Hai, hai."

*

Cousin Shahid consents to have the wedding, albeit with extreme reluctance and only when Jerry Noggles agrees to be converted to Islam. According to Parveen, Mr and Mrs Noggles stubbornly resist the idea, insisting they have their own religious affiliations and it isn't fair that their son be asked to give up the religion of his forefathers. Before long, the argument between the Noggles and the Hussains turns ugly in the Hussain living room in Edison.

In the next room, Phupi Khadija, who has been in New Jersey only a few hours, is tossing on live coals. If she can have her way, she'd will come out and tell the Noggles to keep their church as well as their son. This Zenab receives directly from her. Luckily, Maryam, who is with her at the time, prevents her from making any drastic moves that she would regret afterward.

"She was acting like one of those old crones in Indian films, Phupi Zenab, those grumpy mothers-in-law," Maryam informs Zenab in a confused, bewildered tone.

Finally, after nearly two hours of heated exchange, Jerry surprises everyone by suddenly jumping up from his chair and proclaiming, "If that's what I have to do to marry her, that's what I'll do!"

"Maryam covered her mouth in excitement," Phupi Khadija says breathlessly, adding, "I swear that his voice resounded in Shahid's living room like an evocation in a qazi's sermon, it was as though Allah had spoken through the boy. A conversion will earn them all a reward in heaven." Without waiting for Zenab's reaction to all this she continues emphatically, "All is not lost, after all."

The name chosen for Shahid's prospective son-in-law is Tariq Hasan. Phupi Khadija advises he should be called Kazim Ali after the girl's grandfather, especially since his soul is bound to be troubled and will need appeasement, but Maryam will not agree.

Phupi Khadija is dismayed. "She said her friends can pronounce Tariq Hasan easily. Can you imagine deciding on a name because your friends can pronounce it easily? Hai, hai, what is the world coming to?"

Dr Shah, a pediatrician who doubled as maulavi sahib when the occasion called for it, performs the conversion ceremony a day before the wedding. By that time Phupi Khadija has learned to say, in a halting tone thick with an accent, "How are you?" "I am well," and "Thank you." Since she has been warned about not mussing Jerry's hair when she patted him on the head, she pats him on the back instead when he is brought to her to say "Salaamalekum."

On the phone she says, "He is not so bad-looking, Zenab, and his hair is quite dark, and he's very tall." Phupi Khadija speaks with some satisfaction. "But something troubles me and I don't know what it is."

"Too late for that now Phupi ji," Zenab clucks, "Kamal will have to marry someone else."

"No, no, girl it's not that, it's something else." She sounds fretful.

"Well, you've put your head in the mill, why fear the mortars now?" Zenab uses one of her aunt's favorite adages. She is tempted to add, "Who can quarrel with fate?"

In August, soon after a whole week of rains that fall with the ferocity of summer monsoons in Lahore, the wedding reception takes place at Three Oaks, a wedding hall, less expensive than a hotel. More private, someone says, we can do what we want and there's no one else to wander into our area and wonder if there's some primitive ritual in progress.

The women, Shahid's cousins, aunts, friends' wives, all sit together, mingling a convention still not mastered even though most of them have had the opportunity to learn for over fifteen years. But to Zenab's surprise Phupi Khadija is intent on moving about, like a grande dame of the family, her heavy bulk extended before her like the protective wall of a fortress, a smile, that Zenab feels is forced, mapped gallantly across her face.

The wedding cake, Jerry's contribution to the reception, is four tiers high. Rows of pink and yellow roses adorn each tier, and on the top, precariously balanced under an arbor of tiny white plastic flowers are bride and groom dolls that resemble Ken and Barbie.

"Tariq insisted we must have a cake. Why not, I said. Where we've done so much, what's the harm with one more thing? Is it not pretty?" Phupi Khadija is explaining the presence of the wedding cake to a group of elderly women who are scrutinizing it as if it is some bizarre object that withstood recognition. But she can't explain away the white of Maryam's wedding gown. "Yesterday, for the nikah ceremony she wore a red gharara and the jewelry Parveen had set aside for her specially, but today she insisted on . . . on this. There are some customs we don't understand," she offers lamely, attempting to illuminate and rationalize. "Everyone knows white is the color of mourning, a bad omen for a bride, but do you think these young people pay any heed to their elders any more?"

"But Khala, fashions have changed," interjects Farwa, a cousin's teenage daughter. She is wearing an off-white organza heavily embroidered in gold, a diaphanous dupatta dangling stiffly from her shoulders. "Nowadays the girls don't want to wear bright, gaudy reds at their wedding."

"Such nonsense!" Phupi Khadija retorts. "Tomorrow they will say they want to hold hands with their grooms in public in front of everyone. I say, can't they wait a few hours until they are alone? Such impatience!"

During a lengthy photo session with Jerry's best man and the four bridesmaids, who wear lilac and pink gowns with large bows in the back, Jerry suddenly leans over and kisses Maryam on the lips. All the women at Zenab's table gasp. A corner of her blue chiffon dupatta lifted in her hand, Phupi Khadija covers her eyes in shock, and some of the younger girls, observing her reaction, break into giggles.

Jerry is nearly as tall as Kamal, who, unruffled by his mother's distress over the kiss, or the loss of Maryam to an American, chats boisterously with the best man, a fair-haired, chubby boy with a laugh that goes spilling across the length of the entire hall and makes people sit up and take note. Both Jerry and Kamal have mustaches, but Jerry's sits neatly on his upper lip like fuzz compared to Kamal's which flaps over his mouth like a crow's wing.

"Shahid warned him to observe our customs for the sake of our guests," Phupi Khadija mumbles, "he agreed and now he is going back on his word." Agitated, she looks around for Shahid. Mercifully, he is nowhere in sight.

"Phupi ji, don't worry, he's her husband now, the nikah took place yesterday, actually they've been husband and wife for a whole day." Zenab makes an attempt to placate her, but she continues to scowl unhappily.

To Zenab's relief, dinner is announced a few minutes later. Phupi Khadija, frowning still, rises from her chair, then sits down. The in-laws are to be served first.

Earlier, when the menu was being planned, one of Shahid's brothers had suggested Shalimar Catering be asked to go easy on the red chilies and the garam masala in the korma and the spinach and beef dish. Phupi Khadija immediately protested: "Everything will taste like hospital food, bland and unpalatable, the community's going to go home feeling nauseated and the next day everyone will be saying how bad the food was at Shahid's daughter's wedding. Would the boy's family temper their food for us?" No one could answer that with a positive yes.

"Shalimar's been catering in New York and New Jersey and everywhere else for a long time," Shahid, exasperated with the argument over food, finally spoke up. "They'll know what to do." And the matter of the red chilies was put to rest.

Weddings. Standing at the table with the aroma of garam masala from the korma and the fragrance of the saffron in biryani wafting into her nose, Zenab remembers the weddings she attended in Lahore as a young girl. Always, there was a run for the largest pieces of chicken floating in the gravy, and later a scramble to get to the cool, sweet, firni in the tiny round ocher-colored earthen plates. Spoons forgotten and ignored, the children used their fingers to lift globs of chilled rice pudding into their mouths, closely scraping the surface of the plate to reach beneath to the last of the sweet, thin, white layer. Sometimes, impatient and adventurous, the youngest among them would venture to go one step further and quickly lick the plate.

When the cutting of the cake is announced, some children, girls in brightly colored, gold embroidered shalwar and kameez suits, run, shouting, "Cake! Cake!" Another exodus begins, this time toward the cake. A voice carries over the din, perhaps it is Kamal or one of the other cousins, calling for pictures of the bride and groom with Shahid and Parveen. Zenab and the others push them toward their daughter and son-in-law while Phupi Khadija grumbles that this is all unnecessary.

Parveen squirms awkwardly and Shahid, a stiff smile frozen on his lips, moves forward awkwardly. Finally Parveen adjusts the dupatta on her shoulders, Shahid nervously runs a hand through his hair. There are deep circles under Parveen's eyes and the smile that engages her lips momentarily at Kamal's insistence is tense.

"They should leave now, the bride and groom," Zenab hears her aunt murmur behind her. "Something might go wrong and then where will we be?"

Given her state of mind Zenab is beginning to think she might be right. But their guests don't appear to be ready to leave as yet. The ceremony with the cake has imbued them with lively energy. Suddenly animated, they smile and make jokes, talking noisily as they are served large, white, fluffy slices of cake. The young bridesmaids, Maryam's college friends, their short, light hair bobbing as they throw back their heads to laugh, flirt openly with the best man. Zenab catches a glimpse of Kamal conversing with one of them, a tall, sprightly girl with an easy smile, and she can see he is taking pictures of her wherever she goes. Jerry keeps his arm around Maryam and she leans toward him slightly as if swayed by a strong wind. The sequins on the tiny white florets on the lace of the veil above her forehead glimmer like drops of dew when they catch the light, and her pale skin shines like freshly peeled almonds.

Back in their seats, with cups of tea cradled in their palms and like an enrapt audience glued to a soap opera, Zenab, Parveen's younger sister, Yasmin, Phupi Khadija and the other ladies in their group, watch this drama of unfamiliar exuberance and youthful gaiety unfold. Phupi Khadija is seated next to Zenab. It is past eleven. She is tired and is leaning back heavily in her chair, ignoring the dupatta that slips off her head and hangs limply from her shoulders. She sighs constantly. Zenab draws her attention to the forgotten cup of tea before her on the table.

"You tea is getting cold, Phupi ji," she reminds her.

"Can you think of nothing but tea?" Her aunt snaps at her. "I will not be able to sleep tonight, for many nights maybe."

"But Phupi ji," Zenab protests, "everything is all right now. Jerry is Tariq Hasan and the bride and groom are so happy, just look at them."

Instead of responding to her niece's remark, she gets up from her chair suddenly, tipping the chair as she rises so that it falls back with a loud thud, and says, "I wonder where Parveen is, I must find her."

With a flick of her hand she pushes the dupatta back over her head again and starts walking away from Zenab.

"Phupi ji, wait, where are you going?" Zenab throws up her hands in despair to the accompaniment of chuckles and head-shaking from Yasmin, abandons her half-finished tea and speeds after her aunt.

The Noggles' guests are lining up to say goodbye to Maryam and her husband. Parveen is nowhere about.

"Phupi Khadija, Parveen is probably taking care of some last minute chores before she sends Maryam off." Firmly Zenab grasps her elbow and propels her away from the crowd that is rapidly forming around the bride and groom like rain clouds gathering before a storm. The girls sre laughing, and Zenab sees Maryam raise her bouquet. Some of the nieces and their friends also come forward excitedly. "Catch it! Catch it!" Yasmin's daughter, Farwa whispers in her cousins's ear who turns and says, with a mischievous grin, "Why don't you catch it?"

"Come with me, there's something I have to tell you." Phupi Khadija's voice creeps up on Zenab from behind as she pauses to witness the tossing of the bride's bouquet.

"What is it?" The tone of her voice is alarming and Zenab decides to forego participation in the last minute jollity.

"Girl," she lowers her head and mutters into her niece's ear. "No one has guessed as yet, but when the truth dawns on people, we won't be able to lift our heads in the community. Ya Allah!" Her eyes well and in another instant large tears spill over her leathery cheeks like a river overriding its banks.

Zenab feels goose pimples stir on her skin; her heart pounds in her chest as if she has seen a ghost.

"What is it Phupi ji?" she asks hoarsely. Had someone gossiped in her presence, said something about Maryam and Jerry, that they had been sleeping together perhaps? But she has been with her nearly all evening, there has been no such talk, at least none that she knows of. Zenab's heart races.

Phupi Khadija's face is ashen. "Poor Kazim Ali's soul—hai, hai, such torment! This wretched girl, why could she not marry my Kamal?"

So that's what it is. Zenab's mind suddenly goes blank with relief. Her aunt is indulging in last minute regret. Poor Phupi ji. "Phupi Khadija, it's too late for that now, don't get upset. This isn't good for Parveen, you know, to see you like this." She places an arm around her. "There's Parveen over there, let's go and say goodbye to Maryam together."

Parveen and Maryam are hugging. Zenab's head buzzes with the strains of Shamshad Begum's quavering, dulcet voice:

Chor babul ka ghar mohe pi ke nagar aaj jaana para

Today I had to leave my father's house
To my beloved's domain I had to go.

It is a time for solemnity. Giving away a daughter is the hardest thing parents ever do, and it doesn't matter where you are and who you are giving her away to. Kamal hands Shahid a copy of the Koran which will be lifted high so the newly married couple can walk out under it. Parveen begins to sob violently while Shahid stands next to her with a stoical expression on his face, the Koran held to his chest tightly as if in an embrace. Jerry has moved to the entrance with his parents and best man. All four of them look distraught and puzzled.

Sang sakhiyun ke bachpan bitaati thi mein
Khel gurion ka hans hans rachaati thi mein

I spent my childhood with my friends,
Happily I celebrated the weddings of my dolls.

Phupi Khadija pulls Zenab by the arm. "No, no Zenab, you don't understand," she whispers fiercely, spit flying from her mouth. "It's something else.

Yeh thaa jhuta nagar isliye chor kar mohe jaana para
Aaj jana para

This was a false world so I had to leave it
I had to go, today I had to go.

"Something else? What?" Zenab brushes tears from her cheek.

"Tell me, girl, what good is a conversion? Saying the kalima, saying la illaha illalah Muhammadur rasulallah is not enough. There are other things a Muslim is required to do." She shakes Zenab's arm again and waves a finger ominously in her face.

Sab se mun mor ka
mohe jaana para

Turning away from everyone,
I had to go.

What other things? Zenab thinks wildly. Of course there are other things, but none as important as the conversion. What does she mean? Zenab stares blankly at her aunt.

"What about circumcision? Do you know we are sending off Shahid's daughter with a man who is not circumcised? What about that, girl?" Phupi Khadija faces her niece squarely and raises a questioning hand.

Circumcision? Zenab gapes aghast at her aunt's small, plump hand, then at the heavy, solid gold bracelets that she is saving for Kamal's bride. Circumcision? The constriction in her throat and the moisture that has gathered in her eyes due to Parveen's sobbing and the sadness of the occasion of a young girl's departure from her parents' home, suddenly seems quite ridiculous in view of the images Phupi Khadija's query has generated. Foolishly she stares at her aunt, whose face at that moment looks uncannily like her own mother's countenance.

Dola aya piya kaa sakhi mein chali

My beloved's palanquin is here
My childhood friend, I go now.

"But Phupi ji," Zenab founders weakly, "all is not lost, is it?"

Song of My Mother

Today, she is in my kitchen. Tall still, her lean and shrunken face mapped with lines too fine to count, her small black eyes sunk deep into their sockets, she cradles an emerald green karela in the palm of her hand, her fingers closing over the gourd gently, as if it were a child's face she is stroking.

"You haven't been patient, Zenab," she says with a shake of her head, her eyes clouded just as they are when she expresses disappointment at being alone in Lahore. "Your children leave to go to another country and you putter around in a big, silent house all day long wondering why you're alone." It is not to me she will say this, it will be to someone else, a guest, a relative, a friend's mother. As a matter of fact, she will avoid looking at me so that I may not observe the reproof in her eyes.

She sighs.

"It isn't me," I protest, "it's the karela."

"You have to prepare the karela properly if you want the bitterness to go away." Tiny strands of grey hair, playing truant from her long, thin plait, have wandered on her furrowed brow, floating across the darkness of her skin like faint brush strokes.

I cannot tell her that often, beleaguered by memory's sharp resonance, I have tried to cook karelas her way. The words, reeking of failure, sit on my tongue like the bitter aftertaste of karelas that have been done in a hurry. Long and hard I had labored, until my hands ached and my fingers became numb, and then a full day the smooth-skinned gourds sat in a colander while I waited; much later I realized I had forgotten the salt and so when the rinds were sharp and acrid still, I shrugged and thought, ah, it's because I forgot to use the salt. How could I tell her I had neglected to use salt before I washed the skins? She would look at me in disbelief, then, curling her fine eyebrows, ask, in a soft voice tinged with a hint of a reprimand, how could you forget something so important?

"Amma, karelas in Lahore are different," I say bravely, "these come from Mexico and God knows where else, and look, " I point accusingly, "look how large the raised bumps are on these. How can you expect them to turn out like the ones from your garden?"

Her garden is in Lahore. There the karelas are small, delicate in shape and fine-skinned. But this afternoon she is in my town, a small New England town where summer recklessly crowds life into foliage with such abandon that the blue of the sky and the brown of the earth assume distant, foggy faces. And here, even though summer temperatures may rise to a hundred, karelas cannot grow. Summer is too short a season, too rabid in its abundance, too impatient.

"Zenab, wait, I'll show you," she says, a small, bony hand reaching for the vegetable knife. "You can get the same results from this karela, only you must know what to do."

Silently I watch as she pulls the plastic colander toward her and begins scraping the thick nodular skin of the gourd in her hand with a slow, rhythmic movement. Khrach, khrach, khrach. Tiny sparks of icy cold juice fly off in all directions, a speck of green lands on Amma's hollowed cheek and sits there like a bead. Her eyes are lowered, her brows are curled, her mouth set tightly in concentration. Khrach, khrach, khrach.

The process of scraping the karelas is not new to me. I grew up watching my aunts do it too, every step of the ritual is deeply etched in my memory. I remember the cool, wet sensation of the juice as it flew into my face, the sharp acrid aroma of the skins combining with the smoke from my grandmother's hookah and filling my nose until I could smell nothing else, the brisk chatter of conversation interjected with laughter and head-slapping gestures that passed between my aunts, Amma and my grandmother, the picture of the naked, cone-shaped vegetables after they had been fully cleaned, each smooth and clear like a baby's behind, and myself, a girl-child who had no taste for such a bitter vegetable.

Next, she slices them and disgorges the seeds which, if they are swelled and orange toned, predict an overripe vegetable and thus are cause for dismay. Small and bottle green today, they spill out from Amma's hand and form a mound in the colander. She peers at them closely.

"At one time I used to fry them and toss them in with the rinds," Amma says, always reluctant to throw out what may have even the most insignificant use. "But let's not worry about that now." She has begun to cut up the slices into narrow bands.

Birds, blue feathered and red breasted, are creating a din. I think I also hear the plaintive kuhoo, kuhoo, kuhoo of a cuckoo in a tree out-side my kitchen window. The sun, visible only as brightness filtering through thickly leaved trees, is off on its way to dip into a horizon we can only imagine exists somewhere behind the jungle of woods at the western boundary of our lawn. The air is cooler; a quiet breeze blows strands of hair into Amma's face as she stands at the kitchen window, ready now to wash and rub the rinds. Turning the tap on, she lets the water run through her fingers and onto the karela skins in her colan-der. Then she bends and, taking handfuls between the palms of her hands, rubs them vigorously, energetically, until she is out of breath. Tiny beads of perspiration mark her forehead and there is a film of moisture on her upper lip.

"Let me do this," I say, placing my hand on her arm.

She shakes her head without pausing for a moment in her endeav-ors.

117

We dry the rinds with a paper towel and Amma sprinkles salt on them. Now they must sit in the colander for an hour at least.

The kettle whistles. I get up and make a pot of tea. She sits down at the kitchen table and wipes her face with her dupatta. A vein pulsates agitatedly in her neck, just where the long keloid scar from her by-pass begins.

"Make sure the milk is boiling," she says as I remove the milk jug from the microwave. Quickly I slip it in for another ten seconds. It boils over.

An hour later she washes the skins again, rubbing them down vig-orously once more. All the salt has to be removed. Another patting with paper towels follows. I pour oil from a small cup into the frying pan and wait for it to heat. Amma drops in the skins. They sizzle. A bitter-sweet smell fills the kitchen.

"The idea is not to deep fry," she says, "just have the normal amount of oil you would have to cook any other vegetable." She turns the pieces around with a wooden spatula, watching the pan intently, keeping a close eye on them as they gradually darken, first to a ginger tinged orange, then brown.

I have already sliced one large onion, diced a tomato and chopped two long, slender, dark green chilies into tiny bits. Ground coriander and sharply pointed cumin seeds have also been set aside on the counter to her right. She does not like peering into the spice rack or rummaging through the bottles there.

She signals with a shake of her head and I drop the onions into the pan. Increasing the heat under the pan, she moves the mixture around. The smell of onions cooking in oil draws water in my mouth. She waits until the whiteness of the onions is dissipated, then throws in a spoonful of cumin seeds and coriander. The gold bangles on her slim wrists, thinned from years of wearing, tinkle as she moves the spatula around, her eyes grow restful, the look in them calm. Tendrils of smoke, thick with the vapor of spices and onions, rise above the pan and move lazily upward. She places the spatula on the counter, leans back, a hand set on her hip, and watches the karelas through half-shut, dreamy eyes. I don't know what she's thinking.

The tomato and the chilies go in next. Gently everything is turned over. A lid is placed on the frying pan. Amma lowers the heat to simmer.

I turn on the light in the kitchen and we return to tea. A second cup for us both. I heat the milk again. Outside the birds are silenced. The sound of an occasional car on the road snaps the evening hush, a cricket breaks into song, Kasim ambles in for orange juice.

"What's for dinner?" he asks, reaching for a glass from the dish rack.

"Karelas," I say.

"Not that bitter stuff again, Mom!" he wails.

Amma purses her lips and sighs.

Ten minutes of simmering and the karelas will be ready. I lift the lid for a quick peek. My face is warmed by a sudden gush of steam. "It's not bitter," I say, "Nanima made it her way. She knows this trick which makes all the bitterness go away."

Kasim looks inquiringly at his grandmother

"Yes," she says, her face breaking into a smile. Stretching out her hand toward him, she draws him into her embrace.

Lost in the Marketplace

Lahore is unlike any other place I've ever seen. Not even on its busiest days are there as many cars on the streets and avenues of New York as there are here, day or night. I sit in my aunt's white Pajero jeep, clutch the edges of my seat, my eyes darting in a hundred different directions, my breath held, mostly in fear, while our somber-faced driver weaves in and out of numerous lines of cars, vans and buses with the careless ease of a gymnast. On the road dense clouds of dust arise without warning. Sometimes you can't see what's inches away from you and then suddenly everything clears and you find you were a hairbreadth's distance from a Toyota or a Suzuki and a collision that could have taken your life in seconds. The trick is in becoming passive.

Today we are travelling with Auntie Zahida to her friend's house where I am to meet a doctor my aunt and my mother think will be just right for me. He is, in the words of Auntie Zahida, "handsome, smart, very intelligent, and a Shia." Well, what more could a girl want, my mother's glance seems to be saying. And a doctor too. "The best part is," Auntie Zahida continues in the judicious tone she has developed after years of successful matchmaking, "he's already passed his USMLE." What a relief, my mother's placid expression informs me,

120

one less thing to worry about.

December is coming to a close, but there hasn't been any rain. Tall trees, tahli, oak, and other broad-leafed varieties I'm not familiar with stand coated with a layer of white dust, like ghosts stilled forever. What was dappled emerald green once is now only an indeterminate, dirty olive. The trunks are muddied brown, and the high bushes along the sides of the road or outside boundary walls, look like bizarre mud sculptures. Puffs of dust made leaden with smog seep in through the chink in the car window and fill my nostrils. I place my dupatta before my nose and imagine what life would be like as a doctor's wife.

"Does he have a mustache?" I ask Auntie Zahida, who surprised at my question, turns to face me from the front seat and wrinkles her brow. "One of those long, black things every Pakistani man has sitting on his upper lip?" I add flippantly in response to her brow-raised astonishment.

"You don't like mustaches?" Auntie Zahida asks fearfully.

"I'm not partial to them. Aren't they like a trademark that's stamped on the men's faces? I'm a male, I'm a Pakistani male, the mustache seems to be crying out." I know Auntie Zahida suspects my heart is not in all this meeting young Pakistani boys business. At her house, earlier that morning, over tea and parathas oozing with butter, she had hinted I exhibit caution.

"You mean not talk too much about the U.S., about the boys we know in college, the way we dress there and everything?" I teased, rolling the crispy layers of the paratha in my plate as if it were a crepe.

"If you've already made up your mind you're not going to like him, I don't think we should have this meeting." Auntie Zahida responded sulkily and looking at Mom, pressed her lips together, rolled her eyes and shook her head.

"No, no I'm only teasing Auntie," I reassured her with a smile, my mouth filled with a taste I didn't want to relinquish. I would never say this aloud, but I had decided to put this meeting down as part of my cultural training. So many Pakistani girls exhibited such a flair for

121

this process, Mom and Auntie Zahida had both done it before me, successfully if Abba was any indication or Uncle Rahman, Auntie Zahida's husband. I could at least go through the motions. I had nothing to lose. Yet.

"Well, he does have a mustache," Auntie Zahida said, looking at me closely as our driver honked at a van angrily, muttering something under his breath, "but it isn't one of those clipped military types, thank God." She slapped my shoulder and laughed. "Mustache is only hair, Farwa, it's not a permanent disfigurement."

This isn't the first time I'm in Lahore, but it's the first time I'm in Lahore and thinking of marriage, or rather, being led to think of marriage. Jeanne, my roommate in Connecticut, can't imagine marrying someone you haven't known extremely well, as in having lived and slept with.

"It's primitive, Farwa, how can you even agree to consider it?" she protested when I told her I was going to Pakistan with my mother to look at boys. "Sounds like you're going shopping or something." She eyed me strangely, as if I had sprouted horns or broken out in a blue rash.

"I'm just agreeing to go through this to make my mother happy. I promised her I'd meet these people, that's all. I'm not going to walk into some stranger's living room, take one look and agree to have a wedding."

"What if he's perfect, I mean by your mother's standards, you know, handsome, rich and all that? What excuse are you going to come up with?"

"I've told Mom I won't be pressured. She understands."

But that's easier said than done. Understanding. Actually I place the blame for much of what's going on at this moment on Marium. She's my cousin, my mother's older sister's daughter and she married an American boy. A non-Muslim boy. A great many parents in the family, mine included, pulled in the fences closer on their daughters. The casually watchful became keenly vigilant. Mom conferred with Auntie Zahida who is my aunt from my father's side and after a flurry of correspondence this trip to Pakistan materialized. Sometimes it's best to go with the flow. Life's too complicated anyway. And Mom knows, and I know too, the fences are like paper cutouts, flimsy and unstable, easily blown away by a strong gust of wind.

I'm dressed in the ajrak shalwar kurta suit I bought at Shararay Boutique yesterday. My Urdu is as polished as it will ever be. I remind myself to use the trick my cousin Marium has espoused from time to time during her travels to Lahore. "Jump into English in mid-sentence if you have the slightest doubt about the correct usage or pronunciation. Everyone thinks it's cute when you mix and match Urdu with English." Looking out the window of the car, I see, in the car on my left, a young girl like myself. Short hair, eyes hidden behind sunglasses, thin, a dab of lipstick on her lips. She looks straight ahead though, being used to driving through this morass no doubt, unperturbed by the dust, the noise of tooting horns, the closeness of humanity. Perhaps she's a new-fangled feminist. I've met a few of those lately, the high-mettled, drop-dupatta, chain-smoking types who'll talk to you endlessly about crimes against women between sips on vodka. "Gloria Steinem has retracted and Erica Jong isn't in anymore," I told one of them who was saying all men are bastards.

Soon the car with my twin looms ahead and another takes its place. Another face, a man and a woman, then another, women and children, men only, then children. On and on, like shots from an experimental, each self-contained, yet connected to the others, incomplete without them. Beyond the cars, on the side of roads are vendors who sell forbidden merchandise—tangy chaat, tongue-whipping hot kababs, dahi-bhalas topped with umber-hued tamarind chutney, round, fragile gol gappas with chick peas and a tart, spicy, watery filling, also curliqued, syrupy jalebis bright like swirls of cadmium orange on a palette—not for me any of this, for I am not a local and coming from a country where everything is so clean and so pure, I must not eat any of this. Who knows what germs are concealed in the murky depths of these wares and what havoc they might cause once they find themselves in the bowels of a foreigner like myself. I gaze longingly at what is forbidden and soon Marium and Jeanne recede into the background, like faint memories of a distant past, their place usurped by the clamor of the city, the masks we all wear when we come here, the warm breath of culture that pants closely against my skin, making it tingle.

*

He's wearing tight Levi jeans, a long-sleeved Polo shirt, his socked feet shod in tan penny-loafers, and his hair, dark, swirling masses of it, is swept back stylishly. He has a long thick mustache that shields his upper lip so you can't tell what wonders lie there. He's stocky. I haven't quite registered everything as yet when, almost magically, there's two of him. A brother, I think, a cousin I'm told later. Secretly I wonder if he's also a candidate, if Auntie Zahida, wily and under-handed, had thought to offer me a choice.

There are other people as well. A sister and more cousins, an aunt who seems to be Auntie Zahida's counterpart at that end, some very young children who are watching an Indian film intently, their small heads lifted reverently toward the TV screen, their mouths half-open in wonderment as Amitabh Bachan trusses about some really foul-looking thugs, exhibiting swift and mean legwork as he leaps and bounds across the screen.

"Children, lower the sound please, " the aunt says and then, look-ing at us, smiles apologetically and explains, "they just love all these fighting scenes."

The children do not move and Auntie Zahida and Amma respond with an understanding smile and shaking of the heads. We edge to-ward the drawing room, all of us, as if we're a caravan in search of an oasis. The two young men follow solemnly with their hands behind their backs and I realize with a sudden feeling of panic I don't know which of the two I'm supposed to be observing.

Large and expansive, bigger than any I've had occasion to be in, the drawing room swallows us. Various sofas, some upholstered in flowered tapestry, others with wooden arms and backs, all large enough to be termed sprawling, are positioned along the walls invitingly. I sit next to Aunt Zahida and the two young men are suddenly on the other side of the room, facing us across a colorful Bokhara carpet and several glass-topped tables decorated with alabaster and crystal vases containing a combination of dried and silk flower arrangements. Amma and the aunt sit together and start talking immediately. Within minutes Auntie Zahida has joined them on the pretext of seeking an answer to a question about the troublesome tailor both she and the aunt use and who has been extremely slow lately. A reshuffling is in progress I realize. The two cousins and the sister quickly come and grab the space vacated by Auntie Zahida and my mother.

"Why don't you people also come and join the girls here? Farwa must have stories about America you'll like to hear." Auntie Zahida waves a hand encouragingly in the direction of the young men, who laugh politely and then, while I watch nervously, saunter over to our side of the room. While they are in the process of traversing the breadth of the Bokhara carpet, my mother, Auntie Zahida and the aunt start chatting vociferously. Before I know what's happened, they've left the room.

What stories?

By now I have made a distinction between the two men. One is brash and smiles whenever our eyes meet, while the other is quite deferential, tries not to look me in the eyes at all. And so I find myself drawn to the fellow with the brash gaze.

"Do you like our city?" he asks as if he owns Lahore.

"This isn't my first visit," I say. "But yes, I love Lahore. I don't think anyone can really dislike Lahore."

"Does it remind you of New York City? I hear you're living quite close to it." He has an accent that I can't place. A little bit of the American twang and some of the British tightness.

"No, I don't think there's any similarity, not in the real sense of the word. Lahore is an Asian city, it has an Asian face."

The two female cousins are leaning forward attentively, watching us closely. The sister however, who had been introduced as Ninee, is content to lean back against the sofa and twirl the bristly, pointed end of her long braid that falls over her right shoulder and into her lap.

"Do you mean the dust and the traffic and the poverty?" He is smiling cynically now, one dark eyebrow raised.

"There's enough traffic in New York as well and quite a bit of poverty too, and no I didn't mean that at all."

"Musa Bhai, she means the historical buildings, the culture of the people, the food." One of the cousins comes to my defense in a sing-song voice and I'm relieved I know his name at least.

"And the geography, the fine workmanship of Pakistani life that emerges once the dust settles down." Musa's companion opens his mouth at last. He's smiling benevolently.

"I'm still waiting to see the fine workmanship," I say, trying to temper the sarcasm that's threatening to creep into my voice. "The dust hasn't quite settled yet."

The two men give each other knowing glances.

"Are there many doctors in your area, Pakistani doctors?" It's the benevolent one. Alas, he's the one I'm supposed to be observing.

"There are Pakistani doctors everywhere Sajjad," the young lady on my right who had been chewing gum fiercely, says with authority. She has short hair that envelops her face in soft curls. Her eyes are small and thickly-lashed and the shallow hollows in her cheeks give her face a mature look. Why isn't Sajjad marrying her, I wonder suspiciously when she begins talking. "And soon you'll be one of them." She giggles meaningfully. She can't be too much younger than me, two years at the most. And she has such a pleasant, smiling face.

"There's a brain drain in our country. All our doctors have gone to the US And now Sajjad is ready to flee." Musa leans back and waves a hand energetically in the air.

Sajjad smiles again, indulgently this time. He's still looking expectantly at me, waiting for an answer to his question. I'm sidetracked.

"Well, I don't see America sending people to recruit doctors from

Pakistan. No one is forcing you to go." My voice doesn't sound my own.

"Those who are out there come back with stories of the wonderful life they're leading there and then we are trapped. We are human after all, and a poor country with not enough to feed our people." He crosses one denim-clad leg over the other, takes out a cigarette from a pack of Gold Leaf which he had been playing with earlier and lights it. The flame from the match momentarily throws into relief the sharp, raw angles of his face.

"Musa, come on now, don't tease Farwa. She's our guest." The young woman with the smiling face admonishes gently. "Farwa, tell me about New York. I've heard so much about it. Is it true people can get mugged and killed there if they're the slightest bit careless?"

"People can get mugged and killed here too if they are careless," Musa says with a loud guffaw. He slaps Sajjad on the shoulder and chuckles again. Sajjad emits a small laugh as well. He doesn't seem to mind that he is one of the trapped people Musa was referring to only a short while ago.

I tell myself I must not be abrasive. No one likes women who speak their mind too often or with force. "New York is like any big city," I begin in the most benign tone I can muster, my eyes travelling over my audience. "So many different kinds of people live there. What's so unique about it is that it's, as you've said, a place where you can get mugged and killed if you're not careful, but it's also a place where you'll find the best of the arts, you know, music, drama, exhibitions, films, everything." Sajjad leans forward attentively. Musa is making whorls of smoke with his mouth. "You would like it." I see the men are disappointed.

An elaborate tea is followed by an even more elaborate dinner and more men appear on the scene, another cousin, an uncle, the aunt's husband, a third young man who is introduced as "Sajjad's friend, Ata'ullah." He has a fierce little beard that's blacker than any black I've ever seen and his mustache sort of zooms across his lips and disappears into the sides of the beard without a trace. He's wearing a very long white kurta with a shalwar and carelessly draped around his lean shoulders is a voluminous black shawl. He's not very talkative and quietly murmurs something in a deep, resonant, about saving Pakistan from western pirates, a comment that elicits another back-slapping, approving guffaw from Musa. Compared to him, Musa and Sajjad look like some watery, ineffectual creatures. He has dark brooding eyes which he keeps pinned to the immediate space before him so that if you happen to trespass that space you'll catch his eye and he yours, otherwise he doesn't seem accessible. His name means "gift of God." I like him right away, more than Musa. I wonder what he does for a living and whether he too feels trapped.

*

"He's not one of the candidates," Auntie Zahida informs me disapprovingly. I hope we haven't wasted all this time, she seems to be saying with her eyes. "He's Sajjad's friend, he's a Sindhi landlord's son, a vadera. They're a law unto themselves and they know nothing about women's rights." She examines my face for further clues.

"Auntie, I was just curious. He was kind of handsome, certainly more handsome than either Sajjad or Musa." I can't resist the jibe. Amma is not with us this afternoon. Perhaps she's letting Auntie Zahida probe without the encumbrance of parental constraints hanging over my head.

"Well, you can't have him Farwa," Auntie Zahida persists, smiling this time. "These boys aren't allowed to marry outside their immediate family or tribe. And he's not Shia."

How strange I think, to have to be in such a hostile environment. And what if one were abducted by such a man? "But what happens if one of them falls in love with an outsider?" I can't bring myself out of the eddying current just yet.

"Farwa, you're supposed to be telling me about Sajjad. What's this nonsense about Ata'ullah? I don't know. Maybe his family will make the girl disappear for good, who knows."

"But Auntie, this is 1994! You mean that this sort of thing still happens here?"

Ata'ullah on a horse, blazing a trail in the Sindh desert, his beloved behind him, clasping his waist with both arms, her head resting against his back as he flees from his tyrannical tribesmen. "Yes, you know it does, here and everywhere else. Now about Sajjad—what were your impressions?"

There's sand in my eyes.

"Sajjad? Oh, yes, he's okay I guess. A little too quiet, I'd say. I think he's overpowered by his friends."

"Well, he's not going to take his friends with him to America after he's married, girl. A wife can channel a husband's interests if she goes about it cleverly. And as for his quietness, I think you are mistaking his politeness for quietness. Why, did you want him to chatter away like a gossipy woman? I don't like men who talk too much, to be honest." Auntie Zahida delivers her lecture and waits patiently for a response.

I'm still wondering about Ata'ullah and what he would do if I went up to him and asked to be taken to his village. Sajjad doesn't interest me. I've decided to let him go. He'll have to find someone else to take him to America.

"Auntie Zahida, you've been such a help. I don't want to sound ungrateful. But you know, I don't think Sajjad and I will be happy together. Truth is, I don't think I like doctors." The expression changes on Auntie Zahida's face. Her lips quiver as if she's suppressing a retort, her eyes no longer seem anxious to meet mine. She sighs.

"Your mother will be disappointed," she says, looking somewhere in the distance. "You know Farwa, good boys are hard to find and you know how anxious your parents are to find you a husband who is an all-rounder."

She's saying this very seriously, as if someone's just died, and I break out into an involuntary laugh. It's the "all-rounder" that does it. She looks hurt and I quickly restrain my amusement.

"Auntie Zahida, please don't get upset. If you're upset, Amma will be too. Just tell her the meeting didn't work out, that . . . well, that I thought he was too plump or something." I place a hand on her arm in an attempt to solicit her endorsement.

She shakes her head despondently. "You mother is not going to like this." Then she holds my gaze stubbornly. "Now tell me girl, this doesn't have anything to do with Ata'ullah, does it? You American girls, who knows what wild thoughts you bring with you. I hope you are not entertaining any silly ideas, are you?" She looks suspiciously at me.

"No, no," I say with a laugh. But the truth of the matter is I can't get Ata'ullah out of my head.

"Well, what about Musa then?" Auntie Zahida's voice cuts into my reverie.

"What?" I'm not sure I've heard her right.

"Musa, what about him? He's a mechanical engineer and comes from an excellent family. His father's a retired judge and his mother is an old friend of mine." Auntie Zahida has girthed her waist and is ready for the next assault.

"You're not serious! Musa? I mean he's a really nice guy, much more lively than Sajjad it's true, but I hadn't thought . . . and he hates America." I'm relieved to find an excuse that has a solid, straight back.

"Oi hoi, all the young men say that at first. Don't you know it's fashionable to hate America? Why, hating America is part of our culture and if we didn't do it we wouldn't be who we are. Don't worry about that. What you have to think about is whether you like him or not." Auntie Zahida leans forward eagerly in her seat.

I didn't know Auntie Zahida had it in her to be so funny. Unfortunately I can't express my amusement openly.

"But he talked energetically about the brain drain and he thinks we trap men here with dreams of a wonderful life in the States. I'm quite sure he means what he says."

In a tent, mewls of wind swirling about us, rapping against the flaps of the tent, Ata'ullah holding me within the fierceness of his gaze, his broad-palmed hand resting on my back, its touch fevered, passionate.

"Oihoi, you are too naive, Farwa, you have a lot to learn about us in this country. " Auntie Zahida laughs merrily, dispelling my dream like the flick of a magician's wand.

Puff!

*

While shopping in Anarkali the next day we run into Zenab Khala who is also visiting Pakistan this time of year. She's buying salim shahi shoes and is alone. I'm with Rabiya, Auntie Zahida's daughter who has promised to show me the dark side of Lahore. She means the parts of this old city not often frequented by people who drive Pajero jeeps. Anarkali Bazaar is one such place.

The bazaar is named after Anarkali, allegedly a dancing girl for whom a Moghul emperor and his mule-headed son, Prince Salim, both nursed a passion, and who according to one legend, was buried alive in a wall on the orders of the frustrated monarch whom Anarkali defied, and according to another legend, was banished. Situated on the outer corner of Anarkali Bazaar, a mausoleum bearing her name now houses the Lahore Museum's Records Office.

Anarkali. A pomegranate bud, blood-red, yearning to flower.

My head humming with visions of unfulfilled love as Rabiya embellishes the story of doomed love, I look around at the crowds milling about us and realize we're surrounded by men. There are women present as well, but the dark-skinned, thickly-mustached men, a great many bearded too, nearly all dressed in shalwar kameez suits, looking like a uniformed army on furlough, appear to dominate the central avenue of the bazaar. In all of this I'm really surprised I have managed to spot Zenab Khala sitting on a bench in this poorly lit, narrow, shoe-lined shop trying on a zari salim shahi. I could have easily missed her. Rabiya and I shout and gesticulate wildly to catch her attention, forgetting we're women.

She wants to know how the "boy-watching" process is coming

along. Everyone jokes about this, one of the most serious topics to be ever contemplated, but that's only because making light of the process diminishes some of its more bizarre properties, making it hum-drum, ordinary, yes, believable. I recount the story of our visit with Sajjad and Musa. I don't withhold the part about Ata'ullah. She bursts into laughter and then both she and Rabiya tease me.

"Let's look for him, Farwa," Zenab Khala says with a warm smile, not remembering that she's an aunt and ought not to be encouraging such recklessness. But then she's different. She's lived in the US for twenty years, but unlike Mom, she's a working woman; she teaches. Of course, she also has no daughters and one of her sons dated a Hindu girl for a long time. The young woman's parents had something to do with the breakup, we were told.

Rabiya agrees we should at least make an effort. "I'll investigate," she offers with a tilt of her head. All this is going on while the shopkeeper is yanking off shoe after shoe from the shelves and placing it before Zenab Khala, who, it seems, has very big feet and can't find a shoe she can fit into comfortably. The shopkeeper, a young man with tired eyes and swirls of black hair, some of it falling carelessly on his forehead, looks wearily at us while we prattle in English. Other customers amble in and perked up just a bit, he turns to them.

We give up on the shoes and Zenab Khala suggests, with a barely suppressed smile of glee, that we have some chaat.

"I know just the place," she gestures with her hand, and we follow.

A gulley off the main bazaar leads us into another maze of streets, covered this time and called, I'm told by the two veteran shoppers at my side, "Bano Bazaar," the woman's bazaar. Suddenly we're engulfed by female shoppers. Dressed in black burkas, wearing white chadors with delicate lace edging, some with dupattas fallen in careless tangles over their shoulders, some, like us, consciously plucking at dupattas to make them stay in place. Young women with eager, excited expressions, older women, wary and watchful, little girls who are wide-eyed and brisk of step. And occasionally a man here and there, often staring with undisguised curiosity. The shopkeepers, sitting cross-legged on the carpeted floors of their shops, surrounded by bales of brilliantly colored, richly textured fabrics, eye the river of females expectantly, some rising up in miniature dances, leaping up with extended hands toward the women, beckoning.

There's such a rush at the chaatwallah's I can easily believe he's offering something no one else has. Women congregate around his stall noisily, many awaiting their plates impatiently, others already hastily spooning chat into their mouths, their faces red and sweaty from the hot chilies, their purdahs and dupattas forgotten as they lift spoonful after spoonful of soft yellow chick peas, thinly sliced, sharp onions, tomatoes, hot green chilies and pieces of potatoes, all doused with a variety of tamarind-laced chutneys and spicy yogurt. Flies hum busily around us and over us, the air is redolent with the piquant aroma of spices and tart tamarind juice, our mouths water.

"Don't tell your mother we had chaat," Rabiya warns as she digs into the pyramid in her plate.

"And if you get sick make sure you come to me," Zenab Khala waffles through a mouthful. "I have something that works much better than Imodium AD"

My mouth is on fire. It's a blazing, wondrous fire that leaves me hot and cold alternately. Like there's heat coursing through all the veins in my body. The tastes tap dance on my palate and burrow into my tongue. The tamarind chutney makes my eyes flutter. Just as I'm about to wipe off with a corner of my dupatta the tiny glob of yogurt that's trickled onto the side of my mouth, I see Ata'ullah.

He doesn't see me right away. But when he does his eyes hold mine for an instant in surprised recognition. Walking alongside him, although it's difficult to see who's with whom because everything and everyone is cheek by jowl in this place, is a tall woman in a white chador. Her face, except for the rectangle of her eyes, is veiled. At first I think he's a figment of my imagination, what with all the stories of Anarkali and then the chaat which is burning me up. But then he looks in my direction again and there's a hint of a smile—yes, just a quick, small turning up of the lip nearly hidden under the inky black mustache. I nudge Zenab Khala with my elbow, kick Rabiya's foot with mine.

"That's him," I whisper fiercely, my cheeks tingling, my tongue wobbling.

He notices our stare and before I can fully recover from the surprise of finding him in this unlikely place and in the company of a woman whose face I cannot see and whose eyes reveal no emotion, he trudges away from us, the woman following closely behind.

"Well Farwa," Zenab Khala says with a rueful shake of her head, "that's probably his wife."

"She could be his sister too," Rabiya says, clanking the spoon in her empty plate, striving to scrape off the last drop of chutney.

"Yes, that's true, but we'll never know, will we?" Zenab Khala gets money out of her bag to pay the chaatwallah.

"Unless we go after him," Rabiya offers with a chortle.

Ata'ullah's companion has slowed him down. She is fingering a length of purple chenille on a bale that is part of an arrangement projecting invitingly from the shop's interior. His back is turned to us. He seems to be ignoring the movement of his female companion's hand. I notice rings, a heavy gold bracelet. The eyes dart from one part of the fabric to another. Then she drops the piece and picks up something else. A red chenille. He hovers, restlessly. Although the two of them are together, there is so little communication between them they could easily pass for strangers standing next to each other. Unimpressed with what she sees, she moves on to the next shop, to another display. The shopkeeper jumps from his place to throw open a bale with a flourish. Ata'ullah walks on as well, but his gait is cautious, as if he can feel our eyes on his back.

This is not how I had imagined him. He's incongruous among these mundane surroundings—a bazaar, women fingering fabric, buying shoes, eating chaat. Standing like a watchman next to a fully veiled woman in a busy section of the cloth market while she shops for chenille, he's curiously out of place. Not once had I imagined him anywhere else except in the desert, on a horseback, the wind gusting through his long, dark hair.

And would I also wear a veil if he and I were together in public? Suddenly I think of Sajjad, the doctor with dreams of America in his head, his heart a wide open space where any young Pakistani American girl could fit easily, and fear clutches at my heart. What if I was alone here, and lost?

Zenaba Khala looks at me. I can see she's weighing Rabiya's remark with all the prodigious experience of her years on one scale and the streak of boldness she's suffered from all her life, in the other.

As we talk, Ata'ullah and his female companion turn a corner and disappear.

"Too late now," Zenaba Khala says with a smile. Her eyes meet mine in sympathy.

Rabiya pats my arm reassuringly, her touch comforting, like a sister's.

"We weren't really going to follow him, were we?" I ask.

"We weren't?" Zenaba Khala says and both she and Rabiya laugh like giddy schoolgirls.

I am uneasy. Zenaba Khala's question rankles in my mind, tossing about as if it meant something. "Oi hoi, be serious," I mutter irately, "why pretend we're brave when we're not."

We come out into Anarkali bazaar again and there's a unanimous decision to first drink some pomegranate juice and then buy a bagful of sweet, syrupy jalebis freshly drained out of a black cauldron filled with bubbling, boiling oil.

Lahore is a marketplace, I think as the cool, tangy pomegranate juice travels down my throat. I'm constantly giving something of myself to it when I'm here, and I take something away each time. I'm never now what I was a minute ago. It changes me, makes me a stranger to myself.